Harvesting Faith

Life on the Changing Prairie

Linda K Hubalek

Harvesting Faith

Life on the Changing Prairie

Linda K. Hubalek

Butterfield Books, Inc.
Lindsborg, Kansas

ISBN-13: **978-1480090231** ISBN-10: **1480090239** (CreateSpace-assigned)

Harvesting Faith
@ 1999 by Linda K. Hubalek
Updated 2012

Publisher's Cataloging in Publication
(Provided by Quality Books Inc.)
Hubalek, Linda K.
Harvesting faith: life on the changing prairie /
Linda K. Hubalek. --1st ed.
p. cm. --(Planting dreams series)
Includes bibliographical references.
LCCN: 99-95231
Original: ISBN-10: 1-886652-13-9. ISBN-13: 978-1-886652-13-2

1. Johnson, Charlotta, 1844-1919--Fiction. 2. Swedish Americans-- Kansas--Fiction. 3. Farm life--Kansas--Fiction. 4. Grandmothers--Kansas-- Fiction. I. Title. II. Series: Hubalek, Linda K. Planting dreams series; Bk. 3.
PS3558.U19H37 1999 813'.54

QB199-1168

For an order blank for the Butterfield Books' series, please look in the back of this book, or log onto www.LindaHubalek.com. If you wish to contact the publisher or author, please email to staff@butterfieldbooks.com, or address letters to Butterfield Books, Inc., PO Box 407, Lindsborg KS 67456. Please include a SASE for reply.

To the women who forged the fields
to feed their children

Books by Linda K. Hubalek

Butter in the Well
Prärieblomman
Egg Gravy
Looking Back
Trail of Thread
Thimble of Soil
Stitch of Courage
Planting Dreams
Cultivating Hope
Harvesting Faith

Acknowledgments

I would like to express my sincerest thanks to everyone, both in America and Sweden, who helped me write the final book in this series. It took time and persuasion to make this book a reality, much as it took faith and patience for the Kansas prairie to become an established farm. I think each turned out well in its own way.

Thanks to all who helped "plant" the seed, "cultivate" the dream, and finish the "harvest."

Tack så mycket.

Linda Katherine Johnson Hubalek

Table of Contents

Johnson Family Chart

Parents

Samuel Frederick (July 29, 1836 to Oct. 25, 1919)

Christina Charlotta (Dec.15, 1844 to Sept.13, 1919)

Children

1. **Carl Johan Oscar Johnson** (1864-1935)
wife: **Albertina Carolina Anderson** (1865-1961)
   1. Theodore Nathanial Johnson (1893-1981)
   2. Edgar Bernard Johnson (1897-1969)
   3. Hazel Alvira Johnson (1901-1935)
   4. Elmer Lawrence Johnson (1906-2001)

2. **Emelia Christina Johnson** (1866-1943)
husband: **Constans W. Larson** (1861-1907)
   1. Adelia Larson (1897-1973)

3. **Josefina Matilda Johnson** (1868-1870)

4. **Axel Frithiop Johnson** (1870-1870)

5. **Luther Gilbert Johnson** (1873-1959)
wife: **Esther Miller** (1878-1942)

6. **Theodore Emanuel Johnson** (1876-1884)

7. **Esther Josephina Johnson** (1878-1963)
husband: **Abraham Thelander** (1871-1931)

8. **Almeda Maria Johnson** (1880-1884)

9. **Joseph Nathanial Johnson** (1884-1933)

10. **Herbert Theophilus Johnson** (1886-1981)

Foreword

In this third book in the *Planting Dreams* series, I have my great-great-grandmother, Charlotta Johnson, recall the events that shaped her family's destiny as she says farewell to her mortal life. A mixture of fact and fiction, this book reviews what happened to her family as her children reached adulthood and had families of their own.

I toured Sweden this summer, traveled along a smooth ribbon of surfaced highway through Småland, the province that my ancestors left in 1868. Passing down the road at our modern pace, I wondered if I was viewing the same scenery that they had seen in their everyday lives in their community. Did my ancestors travel down this same road when it was probably no more than a slight trail zigzagging through the forest?

Did I pass the patch of land where they toiled to clear rock so they could plant grain? Is it still in use, or has the forest reclaimed what they had worked so hard to open?

I compared their homeland to the Kansas prairie they chose for their new home in America. The Swedish countryside was hilly, forested with pine and littered with rocks, from the size of my fist to boulders as large as houses. I'm sure my ancestors missed the canopy of green overhead and the shelter it provided, but the freedom from the rocky landscape must have been a relief.

Centuries-old farm compounds are still being lived in. Which one was home for my family? In which summer meadow did my grandmother tend to her cows? Where were my ancestors in this landscape when they planned their departure to America?

Churches still stand, looking much as they did in the 1800s and some for centuries before that. I walked the dirt paths to the churches and down the aisles to the pews within. Had my footsteps followed theirs, did my hand touch the same wooden seats?

Even though the time and setting were more than one hundred years later, I felt my ancestors' ghostly presence in the ancient forests, fields, and buildings that had not changed in centuries.

I made the circle back to Sweden for them and saw what they could never see again themselves. I saw how their lives had changed by leaving Sweden and how it affected the generations to come.

I hope through me and through this book, Charlotta's ghost can relive her past and see the positive things her leaving Sweden did for her family and me.

Tack så mycket, Farmor Charlotta!

L.K.H.

September 13, 1919

Adult children of Samuel and Charlotta Johnson
in front of their parent's home.
Emily, Esther, Herbert, Joseph, (holding dog, Teddy),
daughter-in-law Esther, and Gilbert

The Johnson Family
Gilbert, Esther, Joseph, Oscar, Emily
Samuel, Herbert, and Charlotta

Waiting to Start

Gray light slowly crawls into our bedroom window as the day begins. Objects take shape as the morning creeps up the horizon. The chipped ceramic pitcher and bowl on the wash basin are in the same place they have been for the past forty-plus years. Hat pins, my brush and hand mirror, a handkerchief, show up as a light beam finds the top of our dresser. Sam's jacket is draped across the back of the straight-back chair.

The white lace curtains take turns slightly blowing in and out from the windows on the west and north sides of the room. The breeze is cool and damp this morning. The weather must have changed overnight because until today it has been warm.

Samuel snores softly beside me. The early light hasn't awakened him yet. His shoulders rise and fall with his breathing.

When we were in our prime we would have been up hours by now, had the cows milked, livestock and children fed. At least growing old has granted us the liberty to stay in bed longer. Sometimes I still wake up early though, just because I've done it for so many years.

My eyes strain to focus on the small photograph of our family that rests on the corner of the dresser. The large portrait in the oval frame is hanging in the parlor, but I have always kept a small one in our bedroom also. Even though I cannot see it clearly from here, I know the image by heart. My family; Samuel, the children, and me. We are neatly dressed in our Sunday best. No one is smiling or showing any emotion. We are all holding our breath,

1

staring into the lens of the camera, waiting for it to capture our statues on paper.

It was taken twenty years ago. I didn't realize how old I looked until we received our photos from the photographer. I was fifty-five then, in 1899, but I looked at least a decade older. All the seasons spent working outside on the open prairie took its toll on my skin and aged me past my given years.

Samuel was sixty-three and still a strong man, head of the family, an elder in the community who was called upon for help by the church or neighboring farms. Everyone relied on him.

At the time of this photo, the children ranged in age from Oscar at thirty-five to Herbert, who was almost thirteen. There is such a contrast in their faces. Oscar's face has the worn look of a farmer that has already spent a lifetime in the field. He and and his wife, Albertina, had two children by then.

Even though Oscar stands close to six and a half feet, Emily stands tall beside him. These two have been constant companions since their earliest years in Sweden, and they still remain close. She had been married for five years by then and had two-year old Adelia to look after.

Gilbert was a carefree bachelor of twenty-five when this picture was taken. He had his sights on a farm of his own, but he became Samuel's main help when Oscar left home. He would wait five more years before he settled with a wife on his own land.

Esther, at twenty, was shy and had a quiet manner that sometimes hid her joy for living. She spent her years after school both at home and employed elsewhere.

And then Joseph and Herbert who were still young boys, just finishing their grade school days. Life was so different for them compared to the lives Oscar and Emily had experienced. It seemed that my youngest two were grandchildren instead of children.

I think of my family now. Three married children, one widowed, five grandchildren. And Samuel and I who can no longer keep up with them. When did we grow so old?

I'm reminded of my physical problems again as I try to move in bed. I feel lethargic this morning. My palsy condition has worsened to the point where it is hard for me to move around by myself.

Samuel stirs beside me, and I slowly, painfully turn to face him. I pucker my lips and blow him a kiss. He automatically receives it while responding with a hoarse "Good morning" in our native Swedish tongue. I used to raise up to give him a little kiss on the cheek on every new day, but he settles now for this gesture instead. We've done this every morning for the fifty-seven years we've been together. Will he miss it if I die first?

Time has turned Samuel into an old man. He has lost his towering height and strength and is now overshadowed by his tall children. But his black hair has not been taken over completely by gray, as my own head has.

Samuel's demeanor has changed in the past few years. He's content with letting our sons take over the farm, as long as he can remain here to oversee the land. It's hard to retire a farmer from his farm. I'm not certain that the boys tell him everything that happens, but enough that he still feels that he has a part in the decisions. And some things they still must ask about, because only he knows the answers.

For a while we lived in Lindsborg with Emily and Adelia, but we came back to the farm. Town life was interesting, but we always felt like guests, needing to be dressed up. We missed the solitude of the farm and our Salemsborg neighbors. And when Esther moved back with us, I then had the help I needed to function and care for the rest of the family.

Herbert and Joseph are also still here on the farm. In their thirties, I had hoped they would have found mates by now, but they seem to prefer the bachelor life instead. The other four children married late in life, but I fear these two will become old farmers, never straying far from the land. We've deeded this farm and the land across the road to them, so when our time comes, they will still have this home.

The smell of frying bacon drifts into our bedroom. Esther is preparing our first meal for the day. In some ways it is hard for the two of us to live together again, but it is necessary. I could no longer wash and cook for three men, and she needed a place to stay after she lost her home.

I'm so grateful I can still smell food. If only I didn't have such a hard time chewing and swallowing it. It is so odd. Some functions of my body still work, like my sight and hearing. But I can no longer speak well enough to be understood, and eating is becoming harder every day. I haven't been upstairs for months because my limbs can't make the climb.

It has been hard to adjust to my body's failure. When I first had symptoms two years ago, my doctor told me it was not just old age. It didn't happen instantly, like a stroke, but slowly, over a period of time. He studied his medical books before he guessed it might be a bulbar paralysis because it has affected my speech. There hasn't been much he could do for me as the disease has taken its course.

I had joked to the doctor that I'm like an old milk cow that don't have any teeth left in her head to chew the grass and can no longer gave milk because she can't have a calf.

I'm useless and barren, and too tough to eat.

I was trying to ease his pain, since we both knew there was nothing more he could do for me. I remember Dr. Philbald gave me a curious look, then had a hearty laugh. "Just keep up your spirits, Mrs. Johnson, and enjoy the rest of your life," he said.

Last week when the doctor was here to check on me, he asked, "How's my dear old cow today?" I could do no more than smile at him through my tears. Both the doctor and my family have watched my body slip away but have tried to keep me comfortable.

I've grown depressed about my condition but have faced the fact that I'm in my final months of life as my body slows down.

"Is it Sunday today?" Samuel asks, as he ponders which pair of pants to put on. I have to stop to think. No, it is Saturday. One more day of work, before the Lord's day of rest. My husband answers his own question without looking my way. He is accustomed to me not answering him anymore.

I think of all the years I've worked so hard, wishing for a day of rest. Now that I have no choice, I wish I could do a hard day of physical work again.

Sam comes around to my side of the bed and helps me sit up on the edge. Mornings are still the best for me, so I try to get around until I am forced to recline again. From my position I catch my reflection from the dresser. I see an old lady, shriveled in size with white hair and tired eyes that are set deep in her lined face.

When did my youth start to wane? Probably when we were still in the dugout and I didn't have a mirror to see the transition! Life was hard those first years. But I really didn't feel old until my body started to give out.

"Ready to get up and get dressed, Momma?" Esther asks from our bedroom doorway. I inwardly sigh, remembering when I used to ask her that instead.

The usual talk goes on around the breakfast table. Wondering what the weather will do to the day's projects. Samuel asks Joseph for news within the community because he was out last night.

What has to be done today, what should be done today, and other projects that never seem to get on the list.

This scene has happened every morning for the past fifty-some years, except that Esther is serving the meal, and Joseph and Herbert manage the farm now.

I study these people seated with me around this table. Samuel sits at the west end and I at the east, with children on the sides. The children are now adults, although still sitting in the same chairs as when they were tots. Leaves in the table have been added and taken away as the family grew and then shrank again as they left home.

How will the table arrangement change when Samuel and I are gone? Will the children rearrange their seating, add more members if they marry, or leave our chairs available for company?

It's starting out as an unsettling September day, but I think it will clear by midday. The boys are eager to get started in the field, but I think weather will hold them off until late morning, or even after dinner. There are always enough jobs around the farmyard to keep them busy anyway. And I can think of a few around the house and yard that could use a man's attention, too.

Can we haul in hay today? The last cut of the alfalfa has been cut and turned and is lying in patterned windrows to dry before being brought in from the field. It needs to be gathered on to the hayracks, brought to the barn, and hoisted into the haymow. Samuel cautions Joe that today might be too damp for that project because if it isn't dry, the alfalfa might heat up, combust, and start a fire in the barn. Joseph has heard these same lines every time the hay is down, but his is patient with his father's lapse.

The wheat ground has been plowed and disked once this month. Herbert's morning job is to finish cleaning the manure out of the barn and pens and spreading it on the field. This fertilizer will be harrowed into the soil when the ground is churned one more time right before they plant the seed wheat. They like to wait until about the first of October to plant wheat, but it all depends on the weather. If there is a chance of rain, they'll try to get the seed in the ground to take advantage of the moisture. If it rains hard, though, they'll have to work the ground again to break the crust before planting.

The corn field needs to be checked to see if the plants have started to dry down enough to start shocking. Part of the corn stalks in the corn field will be cut at the base and shocked while they are still green. Later the fodder, both the ears and the stalks, will be fed to the livestock. We used to do it all by hand, but now we use a corn binder pulled by a team of horses that cuts and binds a number of stalks together. The bundles, though, still have to be manually stacked together and tied at the top to form the shock. Then it can stay stored in the field until needed during the winter. When another load is needed for the animals, the men go out with a wagon across the frozen field and bring another supply in.

Another way to preserve the green crop is to bring the stalk bundles right into the farmstead after they are cut and run them through a fodder chopper that cuts the stalks into small pieces. This silage is stored in a metal silo or earthen pit where it ferments in its own juices. None of the crop goes to waste and the cows love the taste.

6

The rest of the crop will have the ears husked off the dried plants that are left standing in the field. This is the last harvest to be brought in and can last until Thanksgiving or past, depending on the weather. The dried kernels will be stored on the cob in a granary bin until needed. It is shelled in small quantities when needed for the pigs.

It's been years since I've been in the fields to do any physical work. I was Samuel's only helper until the children were big enough to add their labor. We worked side by side no matter what the job, be it shucking corn or cleaning the chicken house. The animals and crops had to be cared for, and so I did it, along with taking care of our crude dugout and small children. That was how life was for the first years on this farm.

For some reason this breakfast scene reminds me of a meal one day long ago in my father-in-law's farmhouse in Sweden. I suppose it is because Samuel now resembles his father, Johannes. Every morning Samuel and his father would talk about what needed to be done on the land that day. Sometimes Samuel would listen and take advice from the old man, and other times they would clash on how something should be done. Each generation has new ways of doing things and wants to try them.

The fact is, crops and methods of tending them have changed over the years. We didn't plant wheat in Sweden. When we moved here, we planted spring wheat until the fall variety was introduced. Farmers were reluctant to try it at first, until they found out it did better in our climate.

Johannes threshed grain by cutting the plants by hand, then flailing the seed on the barn floor. Samuel started using machinery for harvest in the 1880s. Now there are hired crews with large threshing machines who come around and harvest the wheat for the whole neighborhood.

Our simple dream of an acreage in America has been fulfilled. We worried so when we couldn't find land in Illinois after we first arrived from Sweden in 1868. We were young and wanted to write to the old folks back home that we had found our dream land immediately. It took another move a year later to Kansas to homestead land before we had a small farm of eighty acres to call our own.

Now our family owns several quarter sections. Our 240 acres on this home place was deeded over to Joseph and Herbert when Samuel turned seventy-five. Oscar and Gilbert own about the same. Esther, although her land is still legally under his husband's name, manages it with help from her nephew, Ted. Emily lives in Lindsborg. Her husband's brothers run the farmland that Emily and Constans once called home.

I always assumed family life would be the same for my children as it had been for me and my parents' generation, but it has not held true for our family. I don't think it is so much because of our children's choices, but society is different now. We married early and started a family right away, automatically expecting a large brood of children. You did not feel right if you weren't blessed with a large number, although all mothers know it was so much more work having more babies to feed and clothe. But children were needed to help with the farm work because they provided manual labor.

Now machinery takes the place of the physical work. Couples choose to have a family or not.

I don't know if it was by choice or fate, but we've only been blessed with five grandchildren. Only Oscar and Emily have had their own children. I've wondered if something I did as a parent made their decision, but it is not something I can ask. And I'm not sure they would be able to answer if I did.

How will the lives of these grandchildren differ from those of my children? I wish I could live long enough to see the change, but I feel that I don't have much time left.

"I'm going out to check some fields with Joe. Want to go?" Samuel asks me, as he turns to Joseph to be sure it's all right he invited me to ride along. Joseph nods a "yes" as he rises from the table. Joseph and Herbert can help me into the back seat of the car easily enough. I'll just stay, tucked into position, until they lift me out again.

I'm pleased they asked. It's been ages since I've toured our land. And I don't know how many more opportunities I'll have.

When did drive-by visits become our way of glimpsing the condition of our fields? It probably became inconvenient to have us out there helping, so one of the boys was delegated to drive us about, like a Sunday outing to view our land holdings. Besides, the boys began to fear for Samuel's safety when he tried to work around machinery. Between his weak eyesight and wobbly knees, he was beyond trying to plant or harvest the crops by himself. It just made sense to keep him active in the decision making but to ease him out of the actual work. I think he was secretly relieved the decision was made for him.

We coast down the road, slowing down now and then to check something up close. The men shout above the noise of the auto to discuss the condition of the fields. Bits of their conversation drift by me with the wind. It's a bit breezy with the top of the car down, but I'm enjoying the sun in my eyes and the breeze tugging at my hat. Joe had put the top down to get me in the car, and he was going to put it back up until I motioned to leave it down.

When Joseph nears the alfalfa field, he pulls by the side of the road and turns off the engine. As we sit in the open car, the sounds of the quiet open prairie return, but the sight and smell is different at this particular spot that when we first came here. A variety of bird songs echoes through the air, but other things have subtly changed. The endless open band of tall grass has been replaced with neat windrows of raked alfalfa.

Looking down over the valley we can see a patchwork of fields offering different colors depending on what was planted there. The dirt road is edged with nodding heads of bright goldenrod. Fifty years ago we didn't see goldenrod—or anything but faint trails through the prairie. We worked so hard to change the prairie, but now I miss its unique beauty.

Joseph and Samuel step out of the car to walk into the field. Each leans over to reach into the windrow and pull out a handful of the cut stems. Almost in unison they squeeze their hands to gauge the moisture and raise them to their noses to smell its sweetness. I've never seen a farmer perform the first gesture without the latter. The aroma of the hay wraps me in it even though I am at the edge of the field. It's one farm smell I look forward to each time the crop is cut during the growing season.

9

When my soul rises to heaven, I think I'll still be able to tell when alfalfa is cut down below because the sweet smell can travel for miles.

Our next stop is beside a field of corn. Streaks of yellow-green in the towering green stalks show that they are starting to dry down. A few lean over now and then, but the corn borer that can knock down a whole field doesn't seem to be abundant this year. If a strong wind rises the stalks will snap off where the borer has worked into the plant. It is devastating to see a perfectly even height across the field one day and see the jagged results of the broken field the next. It just depends on the grub, whether the winter was mild the year before, and whether the stalks have been cleaned out from the previous harvest. If the residue hasn't been hauled out of the field after the corn has been shucked, many farmers will let their livestock out in the field during the winter to eat the remainder.

We were always waiting to start the harvest. But once it began, we couldn't wait to finish it. The stress and worry of getting the crop out of the field added mental work as heavy as the physical labor. Some years harvest went smoothly, and other times we were into the next season before the last of the crop was taken from the field.

The men leave me alone in the car once again and disappear between the rows of stalks. Either the corn varieties are getting taller or the men are getting shorter. I can tell the ears aren't at the same height they used to be, although it can vary with the condition of the crop each year. I also notice that the bottom leaves are drying down and the canopy is shrinking.

How many years ago did I last pick corn by hand? Ten, no, probably more like twenty or thirty years. My sons took over the job, and I worked in the kitchen to prepare all the food the growing boys consumed.

I hear a stalk snap, and a rustling as my men head back to the car. Joseph sets a whole stalk, from tassel to root, on the floor beside me. "Here, Ma. You can shuck this one."

I pull the plant over my lap and caress the stalk to relive the memory of the harvest. The stalks are still firm and green, the leaves are velvety soft, except for the sharp edge of the blade.

We were so eager to harvest the first crops off this land. So often during those first harvests there was too much work and too little sleep. Add the needs of the young family and farm, and I felt overwhelmed. I'd move from constant motion to exhaustion before the last grain was cut. The harvest seasons rolled together some years, and we wouldn't be done with oats and wheat before it was time to cut hay, then sorghum and corn. Then there was planting and tilling in between . . . we've always had busy summers.

I did so much thinking out in the corn field. It was a job a body could do without thinking, leaving the mind to wander on. When we picked together as a family, the children always complained because it took forever for lunch time to arrive, but my mind was always racing ahead and I didn't notice whether I was hungry.

Some days I got more problems solved than bushels picked.

How were the children doing in school? One of the boys was probably struggling with his math lessons the night before.

It was my turn to serve refreshments at the next ladies church meeting. Should I make two cherry pies, or an angel food cake?

I worried about farm expenses. Will the weather cooperate so we can get the entire crop out of the field before the weather turns bad? Will we make enough money off this crop to get us through another year?

What if someone is hurt running the machinery? How would we cope with the injury, the loss of time, the expense, the absence of the extra help in the field?

Many worries were faced and much deep grief wrestled with in the corn field. Tears were shed for grain lost because of weather, for ailing parents I could never see or help, for memories of children buried.

I relived the past when I touched this stalk. I could feel my body passing through the first row of corn, reaching for the first ear and snapping it off the stalk, ripping the husks off with the strength of my hands, flinging it without effort toward the bed of the wagon. Thunk. Thunk.

Two hits? The sound of the car doors slamming brings me back to the present. I am an old lady again holding a stalk of corn.

11

Edgar, Ted, Oscar, Hazel, Elmer and Albertina, circa 1912

Surveying the Crop

"Won't you come in for coffee?" asks Albertina. Joseph starts to answer no, either because he wants to move on or it meant getting me out of the car, but Samuel answers, "Why, sure!" He already has the car door open, waiting for the invitation. I think Joe's plan was to stop in Oscar and Albertina's farm for a just minute, but his time schedule has just been changed.

Was Albertina ready for this, or just being polite? No, any farm wife is ready to set the table with an extra plate or two for a meal. And all good Swedes have forenoon coffee, so the pot is already on the stove. Bread, butter, and jam can make a quick sandwich if cookies aren't available.

Samuel will have his hat off and be seated at her kitchen table before the rest of us wander into the house. He loves his coffee and cookies.

The warm comfortable scent of our favorite brew hangs heavy in the kitchen, along with the aroma of the hot loaves of rye bread she must have pulled from the oven the same time we pulled into their driveway. Melted butter in a little saucepan sits beside the loaves, waiting to be brushed on top of their browned exteriors.

A large table graces the ample kitchen. How many coffees and meals have we shared at this table in the past twenty years? We're just as comfortable in their home as in ours, I'm pleased to think.

Oscar and Albertina's home

I need to stretch my legs a bit so I wander into their dining room before sitting at their kitchen table with the men.

The dining room table, used only for Sunday dinner and company, is covered with a lace tablecloth. The china cupboard against the north wall boasts fine cut glass pieces on its top surface. The walls display portraits of their children at various stages of growing up. Plants sitting in the bay window of this room enjoy the east sunlight early each morning. Extra chairs line the south wall.

The muffled bong of a mantle clock pulls my gaze into the living room that lies to the north of this room. The glass doors that divide these two rooms are open, and I slowly make my way into the room. Light shines through the colored panes of glass that grace the top of the north window, setting off a kaleidoscope of color against the opposite wall. A mahogany settee and matching rocker and chairs make this an elegant parlor. The secretary in the corner is used as a writing desk and place to display Albertina's treasures.

Good times have been shared here over the years as I think of Christmas Eves and simple Sunday afternoons. I thought this house was more room than they needed when they built it, but it was the style, and they could afford it. Secretly I'm happy that my son could build such a nice home for his wife and family.

I feel a large hand on my shoulder. I was immersed in my thoughts and didn't hear Oscar come up behind me. "Ready to join us, Momma?" he asks as he gently takes my elbow to guide me back to the kitchen.

I pause in the doorway to soak in the sight of my menfolk

Oscar, Ted, Edgar, and Albertina

seated around the table, all ready for another meal!

After getting me seated, Oscar gingerly takes a hot loaf out of a bread tin, drops it on a wooden board in the middle of the table, and attempts to cut it while it is too hot, resulting in mashed hunks. A few minutes of cooling time would make it easier to slice into even pieces, but that thought apparently didn't occur to him. The three men dip the bread into the pan of butter and enjoy the first slice before Albertina has time to place plates in front of them. There will be a few spots of butter to wash out of the tablecloth after this morning coffee. But Albertina takes it in stride and doesn't scold because she knows there are habits the men won't break.

Albertina takes four tins of treats out of the cupboard. Two types of cookies, one cracker, and rusks. She always has sugar cookies available for company.

With simple ease my daughter-in-law sets out enough food to make this our noon meal instead of a simple coffee break, all the while adding to the table conversation.

Albertina

"Any burnt sugar cake this morning?" Samuel asks hopefully. Her recipe is a family favorite. "No, I'm sorry, Sam. You'll have to come back for afternoon coffee for that," she replies.

Oh, how my own mouth was watering for a piece. So many foods are hard for me to eat, but that cake and rich frosting always slide down so easily. Now I'll be hungry for it all day.

Albertina was a good match for my son. She and Oscar were wed in 1892 and have spent their entire married life on this farm. Albertina was born in Sweden and did not travel to America until 1884, when she was nineteen. Albertina worked in the broomcorn fields until she found a job as a housekeeper in Salina.

She and Oscar met because her two brothers, John and Alfred Anderson, had come earlier from Sweden and settled in this area. A sister, Beda, stayed in Sweden, but they keep in touch. Her parents came over for a yearlong visit not too many years ago, so we enjoyed getting to know them.

Oscar and Albertina started house-

Their wedding, March 17, 1892

16

keeping in the little house that was already on this land, then built this big two-and-a-half story house in 1905. It has a large kitchen, separate dining room with a bay window, living room, and downstairs bedroom. Upstairs boasts four bedrooms, with an attic above. Outside are two porches, one on the north that leads into the living room and the other on the south for the kitchen. They have planted an orchard on the east and lilacs and shade trees around it.

I take a good look across the table at Oscar. Age is taking its toll on him. He turned fifty-five this last January. When did my first-born son

Oscar

grow old? His chiseled face is dark red from the summer's work. Oscar's hair has shades of gray blended in with the black. His right hand, injured some years ago in the wheat binder, waves in the air with his gestures. It has shriveled in size compared to his strong left. He is talking to Joe and Sam about the fieldwork, about what stage each field is at in its cycle of growth. Each of us knows what field and location he is talking about by its nickname. So many years have been spent on this homestead, that we know the lay of the land, the type of soil, the drainage and problems of every field.

Samuel asks when Oscar thinks the corn will be dried down enough to start harvest? Has he stopped by to check the alfalfa on the north section? He and Joe have already decided these questions, but Sam wants Oscar's opinion, too.

Samuel has always leaned heavily on our eldest son. Being the first child and boy, Oscar has always had the responsibility of helping us and his younger siblings. I'm sure the load was too

17

heavy for him at times, but he managed silently. He's been so supportive throughout the years.

I wonder. Samuel and I followed our dream to America. What were Oscar's dreams and has he fulfilled them?

He farms several hundred acres of land, his farmstead has grown to include a fairly new house surrounded with shade and fruit trees, barns and outbuildings on a grand scale. His place dwarfs our modest farmstead, I'm proud to say. Oscar and Albertina have done well for themselves and their family.

He had no choice in the decision to move to America. What would his life have been like if we had stayed in Sweden? He would have inherited the land from Samuel's father—if we would have been able to hang on to it through drought and taxes. There would have been no farm ground in the area for expansion as we had here. Starting a new farm on the American prairie was difficult, but at least we had opportunities for growth and freedom here. He wouldn't have had that choice in Sweden.

I do regret taking him away from his two sets of grandparents. He was old enough to know and love them, and he mourned the loss of their contact. Samuel's parents lived with us, so they were part of his daily life. They were the ones who had time to play with and coddle him when Samuel and I were working. My parents, while living farther away, saw us often enough that Oscar and Emily knew them, too.

We have reminisced about our homeland over the years, in passing comments or stories. Sometimes Oscar would add his own comments or ask questions. It is hard to say what Oscar truly remembers or what he thinks is a memory because of our stories.

Of his grandparents, Oscar remembers the smoky aroma of Grandpa Johannes' pipe and the soft texture of the red wool shawl Grandma Cathrina always wore. Simply thinking of those two things can take me back to the house in the Kulla farm, with all its extended memories. The stone fireplace blackened from cooking meals on the hearth, the old straw roof that needed to be rethatched on the barn, the winding path between the boulders going up the hill above the hay meadow. And each one of those thoughts expand another cluster of memories. Good or bad, they are part of my memories that can still be recalled today when hearing one word or smelling an odor that reminds me of a time decades ago.

In some ways I wish we could have stayed longer, so all the children born to us could have shared the memories of Sweden. Oscar was the only one who remembers anything from our former lives. He also remembers little jolts of scenery from our trip across the sea: sea gulls waddling on the deck of the boat, the smell of the sea air, the crowds in New York City, different things that I don't remember. He was seeing things with his four-year-old eyes, with a child's reasoning, and marveling at our adventure. Oscar wasn't afraid of anything on the trip but constantly wondered out loud the whys and hows of everything.

I, on the other hand, was too worried and exhausted to enjoy most of the trip. My mothering instinct was strong as we herded the children through the cities on our trip. We learned in Gothenberg that people generally ignored the bewildered country folk who were passing through on their way to the docked ships in the city's harbor, unless they were wanting to take advantage of them. The same was true for New York when we left the ship. I only relaxed when we were in settled in Illinois among fellow Swedes again.

Then tension mounted again when we started over in Kansas, but the passage of time and persistence paid off for our family. The move was the right one for all of us, but it did affect Oscar's young life.

Oscar's memories of our first years are singed into his mind with dirt, sweat, hard work, and the loss of his siblings. For a while I felt that he blamed Josefina and Axel's deaths on the land. I realized he was just following my anger and grief. But together we all worked through those losses as we built the farmstead.

Laughter around the table brings me back to the present. Some joke must have been told that I didn't hear.

My youngest grandchild, thirteen-year-old Elmer, wanders in from outside. I saw him earlier leading a team of horses into the barn. He's going to be another tall Johnson even before he reaches his full height. Elmer pulls up a chair to join us and reaches for a slice of bread on the board set in the middle of the

Sunflower School, 1903

table. His sister, Hazel, pours him a cup of coffee, into which he pours a generous amount of cream and sugar. It doesn't seem that long ago when I was holding him in my lap, feeding him bits of cookie dipped in coffee.

She also pours another cup because Edgar, washing up, will join us.

Hazel, at eighteen, and Edgar, at twenty-two, still live at home, helping with the household and farm work. Our oldest grandson, Ted, lives on daughter Esther's farmstead. We have watched them all grow over the years from toddlers to young adults, attending their school and church activities. They attended Sunflower School, a mile south of this farm. Ted and Edgar both continued their education with the two-year commercial course at Bethany College in Lindsborg.

Our grandchildren's lives have been so different compared to those of our oldest children. They helped with farm and house chores too, but on an established farm. They had time for recreation that my older children rarely had when they were young.

20

Actually my youngest sons, Joseph and Herbert, are closer to Ted and Edgar in age than to their own siblings. There are only seven years between Herbert and Ted, his nephew, but twenty-two between Herbert and Oscar, his brother. They went to different grade schools but were together for church activities.

The grandchildren have grown so fast. It didn't seem that it happened to my own that way. I still have a hard time grasping that Ted is married. Will his wife, Elsie make me a great-grand-mother before my time here is over?

I can still vividly recall the cold February morning Ted was born. That's been twenty-five, no, twenty-six years ago.

The cold is refreshing as I ease out the back door to give the new parents a little time alone. I lean against the door frame with relief. My breath clouds the air before me as I sigh. Now I can relax a moment and regain my composure.

Thank God that all went well. I've helped many laboring women and done it myself so many times that I automatically do what is necessary. But there is always that joy when the birth is a success and both members are deemed all right.

Dawn has started to creep up the horizon. The soft pink glow of the sky reminds me of the delicate skin of the newborn. Yet one is so big and the other so small.

A sifting of snow blows across the top of my shoe and the white crystals settle in between the lacings of my boot. It disappears into water as I blink my eyes. This new snow that fell last night was barely enough to cover the old crusted layer that has weathered against the buildings. If it warms up today, both could melt into the grass and run into the earth's waiting cracks.

The wind blows tendrils of hair that have escaped my usual tidy bun. I should have picked up my cloak before I headed out the door because the sweat on my neck is turning cold. But right now the biting weather feels good. Warm tears trickle down my cooled cheeks as I grasp this momentous day.

Samuel will be pleased that there is another generation to whom we can pass the name and land.

Oscar arrived at our doorstep shortly after midnight, shouting and rushing through the house into our bedroom, giving us a fright as we bolted up in bed. I thought he was rushing in to rescue us from a burning house. He had been around enough of my births that I was surprised to see him so shaken. But then this was his first child, and Albertina was home alone waiting for his return with help.

The two-mile trip around the section was the quickest I had ever made. After we made the ride in record time, I strongly suggested he stay in the barn and care for the sweaty horse before he came back to the house. Both needed cooling down.

The delivery was normal for a first-time mother, but there is always the worry and pressure of childbirth. She's just had her first child at age twenty-seven. I had four by her age.

I wipe my face with the back of my hand and feel the wetness transfer. I look at my hands and realize that this morning they were the first to touch the second generation of our Johnson family to be born on Kansas land. My first grandchild was born this morning to Albertina and Oscar.

I had cradled him for a moment after I wiped his little pink body and wrapped him in a blanket of flannel. His face scrunched for his first wail of air. I looked for a hint of family resemblance. Does he have a Johnson or Anderson nose? His hair is light brown, not black. There are no brown eyes in either family, so we'll assume they will be blue.

Albertina's sweaty face beamed as I laid the baby in her arms, and she automatically started talking to him. He stopped his crying and looked up toward her voice, recognizing something familiar.

Oscar eased the bedroom door open and soaked in the scene of his new family. The look on his face was pure joy as he headed toward the bed. This moment was between my son and his wife, so I left the house for a little while.

Memories flood back from Oscar's birth. The Kulla farm house in Sweden, my mother assisting. The panic that dissolved to wonder of the child that my mother laid in my arms.

Both mother and grandmother wonder and worry about the same things. Will the child grow up healthy, what will he do for a living, when will he start a family. But it is different, because I will not be the primary care giver who shapes his life. Another set of parents will do that, and I can only hope we did our best to raise our children, so they will do likewise with their offspring.

Now I know how my mother felt. Her role changed from mother to grandmother in an instant.

Oscar opens the door in search of me, steps out into the cold and gives me a tight hug, clinging to me as if he were my little son again. Although he says nothing, I know the emotions he is feeling. The awe and worry of being responsible for a child have sunk in.

He finally releases me, looks down into my face, clears his throat to steady his voice, and says, "I know it's been the family tradition to use the name Johan for the first son, but we've decided to name him Theodore Nathanial, Mamma. I still miss brother Teddy, so I'd like to honor my first-born with his name. Will Poppa be upset?"

I was caught off guard, in an instant reliving my son Teddy's birth and death.

Oscar probably thought I was going to protest since I took more than a second to answer.

"No, Oscar, we'd both be proud for you to use that name."

Time draws me back to the kitchen table, and as my son's face fades back to the present.

"Momma, are you feeling all right?" he asks with concern.

It's hard to tell. I seem to be reliving the past today, detached from the things going on around me in the present. Thinking of births and deaths. Places and events long forgotten over the decades have returned as clear visions. Some joyful, others sad. People long gone are back by my side.

I study my family around me and shudder with the thought of how much longer will I be with them? My eyes well with emotion, and I feel a warm tear slowly trace a path down my cheek.

No, I don't feel all right today. Something is wrong, and with sadness, I think I know what it is.

Constans and Emily's wedding, May 12, 1894

Stalling for Disasters

Discussion turns to other jobs that need to be done. Albertina is getting low on flour. Do I know if Esther needs any? We'll be making a trip to the Lindsborg roller mill next week if you do.

Yes, I think she mentioned she was getting low. The last was ground before this past wheat harvest. We wanted to use up the last of the old grain before the new was brought into the granary.

I used to love watching wheat fields as they waved in the Kansas wind. It reminded me of the prairie grass when we first moved here. It was the same motion of flowing with the wind current, then drifting back when the wind stopped to take its next breath.

When the winter wheat first comes up after fall planting, you can't see it without getting down on your knees to peer close to the ground. Then gradually the brown field turns to a carpet of green until the first hard freeze slows its growth.

You can tell when winter is ready to break into spring because of the slight ripple in the green as the leaves grow. Then warm air and lengthening days raises the wheat stalks from the ground until it forms its seed head in May. The wave deepens as the heads turn from deep to light green, then to a deep gold on bended stem tips, as the kernels dry and grow heavier in weight.

Anticipation of wheat harvest is always high, probably because it is the first major grain to be harvested in the summer. Everyone has a patch of oats to cut first, but those acres are much fewer than the big fields of wheat that everyone plants now.

Bills have been piling up over the winter with farm upkeep and spring planting, so the wheat crop promises cash relief.

Starting in the early part of June, Samuel wore a path down to the wheat field to check the daily progress of the kernels. He'd make the trip every morning before forenoon lunch, hoping to report good news at our break. First he would report that the grain was swelling and starting to mature. Excitement mounted in mid-June when the little kernels filled with their whitish milky fluid. Full ripeness was then only a week or so away.

At this point Samuel would peel back the beards and smash the heads into his palm to expose the golden grain, blow the chaff away, then pop the wheat into his mouth and chew. The kernels needed to be hard enough to be mature, not rock hard so that the wheat heads would shatter out the seed when handled. There was a fine line between too green and too ripe.

Then we would hope the weather would be ready the same time as the wheat. Nothing makes a farmer more sick to his stomach than having wheat ready to cut but then not being able to do so because the field is too muddy to enter.

Samuel and the boys would pull out the horse-drawn binder from the shed, clean it, and repair any worn parts two weeks before the wheat was ready. For weeks before and after the event, harvest was the main topic with the men after church on Sunday. They worried, boasted, and lamented together depending on the preparations, work, and outcome of the yield.

When the wheat was deemed ready, the binder was pulled to the edge of the field. Even if I wasn't helping, I liked to be in the field to watch the team and binder make the first round through the field. More often than not, stops were made to check and adjust parts to make the machinery work properly. But it gave me a sense of accomplishment to see the sickle cut the stalks close to the ground, the webbing pull the cut crop into the machine, the even bundles released and tumbling back onto the stubble field. Of course that was just the first part of the harvest.

Next the bundles were gathered to be stacked into shocks. Six bundles were set upright and one spread over the top to hold the rain out. The children learned their directions in the wheat

Stacking wheat bundles to be threshed

field because the top bundle had to face west to keep the winds from lifting it off and drying out the wheat heads it protected.

The neighborhood would be checkered with wheat shocks until the threshing crew wound its way through the countryside maze.

From then on, wheat harvest became a community event. Men, women, and children all took part in helping the threshers as they set up at each farm. The man who owns the traction engine runs it, but many hands are needed to pool their labor to form the threshing ring. The thresher and the traction engine that powers it with a big belt is set up at a central location at the end of the field or the farmyard. Using their teams of horses, men load the shocks onto the hayracks and haul them to the thresher. The bundles are pitched heads first into the conveyer, where they are threshed to separate the straw from the grain.

One man runs the blower to stack the shredded straw and another packs it down. Someone else drives the horse team under the chute to catch the grain, which pours into the waiting grain wagon. When full it will move on to the granary to be unloaded, and another wagon will take its place.

Of course this all happens during the hottest part of the year. You wish for a breeze to cool your sweat, but then the wind whirls the wheat chaff everywhere, and you are covered with the itchy

Emily

particles. It's even worse if the straw is dirty or moldy. Some nights the men would be hoarse from the dust and from yelling above the machinery, but that was part of harvest.

Children are assigned jobs depending on their ages. The boys who are too young to actually help with harvest are kept busy hauling water from the well to the men in the field. Children help prepare the noon meal for the dozen or more men who will descend into the dining room. They are sent out into the garden to pick beans or whatever is ready to prepare. Chickens had to be caught, butchered, and cleaned for frying. Potatoes peeled, tables set, clean water and towels placed outside for the men to wash up with, babies to entertain. The young ones looked forward to the idea of the threshing crew coming to our farm but soon remembered all the work that came with the extra crew.

The amount of work for a woman depended on whether the threshers were at her house or if she were simply helping that day. I'd be up before the summer's dawn baking bread and pies for the crew. By ten o'clock, the hours of heat from the wood stove made the kitchen almost unbearable. Our clothes were as wet as those of the men who were working in the sweltering sun.

The meal had to be one of the best I prepared the whole year, else word would get around the neighborhood. After several years, most wives were seasoned to threshing crews' appetites and could orchestrate a meal for twenty men. Family members or a neighbor woman or two would help, dropping off a pie or cake to add to the meal.

I sympathized with the young wives trying to prepare these feasts. Most had helped their mothers in the past, but it's different being in command for the first few times. Men might be polite at the table and not comment on scorched potatoes or dry meat, but for the woman it is still embarrassing.

I remember Emily's first dinner for their threshing crew. It went very well, but then she was accustomed to feeding and taking care of many people at one time. She worked in Brookville at a hotel before she married at age twenty-eight, so she handled the crowd with ease. And I remember her husband, Constans, quietly beaming as someone announced that Emily's cherry pie was the best he had tasted in the neighborhood. She had fixed a wonderful dinner for the crew, and he was proud of Emily that day.

Constans Larson. We've known his parents since we were children in Sweden. Constans was born in the same community in Pelarne that Emily was and made the trip to the area with his parents the same year we did. He and Emily knew each other growing up and were going to spend their lives together farming, much the way Sam and I did.

They were married in May of 1894, set up farming in the community to the northwest of us, and were blessed with one daughter, Adelia, three years later.

I also remember the last meal she prepared for the threshing crew. Life changed drastically for my eldest daughter on that harvest day in 1907.

One never realizes how one misstep can alter a family forever.

Emily had just dropped the last chicken drumstick in the frying pan when we heard panicky shouts above the drone of the thresher and engine. I was cutting a cherry pie and stopped to listen. The engine was chocked off, and we heard one man scream in pain. We turned and stared at each other in dread. Oh dear God, I thought, someone is caught in the machine!

Constans

29

Everyone in the house rushed to the door, scared to look but needing to know who was hurt. Whose husband, brother, or father had just been injured?

The men were congregated around someone near the thresher who was waving his arms in the air. In one quick motion, he was hoisted in the air, then lowered to the ground.

"Get a board or door to put him on! Bring an empty wagon around here! Let's get him to the house!"

After too much time, the wagon, with a ring of men surrounding it, slowly made its way toward us. I could see two men kneeling on the bed, steadying a body between them.

They brought Constans in, face down on a wagon sideboard. Instinctively we grabbed the dishes and glasses off the table as they carried him up the steps. The silverware crashed with a glass we forgot to remove as Emily swept the tablecloth off. Constans was conscious but gritting his teeth in pain. Blood had darkened the seat of his pants.

Black smoke from the unattended frying pan drifted into the dining room. Adelia cried for her poppa as I hugged her to my waist. Orders were given to get the doctor, bring scissors to cut off Constans' pants, clear the room. The man who ran the engine was still in charge, barking orders to snap the shaking men into action. Children were sent outside while the women went back into the kitchen to salvage the burned meal. Tears silently left white streaks down several men's faces as the seriousness of the injury was assessed.

Constans had stepped backwards off the thresher and impaled himself on the tines of a pitchfork that had been stuck upright in the ground. The tool punctured his backside.

Emily anxiously wiped his face with her apron until someone brought a bucket of water and a towel. The look he gave Emily sent searing pain deep into my chest. Constans knew he wasn't going to recover, and it must have distressed him to think of leaving Emily and Adelia alone. They both knew that their moments together were fading.

Constans laid lingering in pain until infection took hold in the deep punctures and claimed him a few days later.

The neighborhood was shocked. The church was overflowing with family, friends, and neighbors for his funeral that following Sunday afternoon. Worse still was the fact that Constans was the second son of the Larson family to die within three months. Constans' brother Carl had died in March from an injury that happened at the Smoky Hill Quarry the year before. His injured ankle never healed, even though Carl and his wife traveled to a Chicago hospital to have it treated. Surgery was performed, but not successfully, and Ida came home a widow.

So Emily's life took that same path as well. She left the farm three years later, renting an upstairs apartment in a house across from Bethany College in Lindsborg.

Adelia was ten when it happened. Unlike our other grandchildren who live in the country, she spent her school years in Lindsborg, even attending Bethany's music department. The two have had to live frugally, but they have managed.

Recently, Emily has talked about moving to Salina. I don't know all the reasons, but I think she is hoping that Adelia will have a chance for a job—or a husband who isn't a farmer.

Emily was two when we left Sweden. She worked beside Samuel and me as we built the homestead, knew the fields as well as Oscar, watched the weather ripen or ruin a field of grain. She knew what nature could do, but she couldn't accept life's circumstances when that harvest took her husband. Twelve years later she is still seems angry and seldom comes out to the farm. The land is a bitter reminder of Constans' death.

I wish she would have remarried. I don't know whether she had no prospects or simply turned them away, but Emily was a young woman when the accident happened and could have spent years with another husband, possibly having more children as well. She is missing out on so much by exiling herself from life.

I know I would have hated to be without Sam all these years. Each decade was different for us as we aged. Maybe I would have felt the same as Emily if my circumstances had been the same, but I doubt it. Times were different then. It would have been hard to survive as a widow with so many children. Adults in my younger days remarried to make their lives easier. Often they were unions of necessity, but I know couples who have had a good second marriage despite the original reasons that brought them together.

I just wish life would have provided Emily a second chance.

Emily and Adelia, 1907

Starting the Thresher

Coming home we drive south around Oscar's section, then west to turn north along the road that waves up and down along the bottom edges of the Smoky Hill Buttes. The nearest span of hills rises sharply to the west. The morning light make its sides look like a rolling carpet of grass, with an occasional cropping of sandstone. About a mile south of our place the hills stop, but start again further north of us.

We travel along a variety of crops as we pass neighbors fields. Corn, milo, and cane sorghum. Another field has been plowed and disked, ready to be planted into wheat. A patch of native prairie, cut, dried, and hauled into a barn during the summer has grown back to form a shorter version of prairie sea.

The variety of crops grown in our area have increased and changed over the years.

Broom corn was a big industry our first years. Factories in the area's largest towns bought our crop to make brooms. It was grown in Illinois where many of these families stopped for a few years, so it was natural to try it here. It was our first cash crop that we sold. It also provided jobs for many of the first young immigrants who landed in Kansas. It took a lot of hand labor to harvest and process it. Times have changed, and it's not widely seen anymore as wheat is our main crop now.

Besides being sold as a cash crop, wheat also is used for chicken feed and flour. Everyone planted spring wheat until immigrants from Russia introduced hard winter wheat to Kansas in the 1870s. Although wheat has become the main source of our flour, most Swedes still have a small patch of rye so we can grind the grain for our rye bread. Oat flour is a favorite for some, but it is grown mainly to supply feed for our work horses.

We pass a rock fence made of red sandstone that lines one field. They are made the same way we stacked them in Sweden, although because of the area, fences in the old country were made of different rock.

That rock fence is the only thing that is similar between our farming community here and our old home. I became homesick every time I passed it when the farmer first built it. Later it served as a fond memory of our past and a reminder of why we left rocky Sweden in the first place.

Large fields blanket our community here; they are not small patches cut among the trees and rocks. I grew to love the vast open spaces, but it took time. I remember longing for the shelter of a mature tree the first years. We had to travel miles to the Smoky Hill River to see one, and believe me those few trees were visited by many Swedes in this area.

Climate was one of the biggest adjustments we had to make. Everything from temperature, amount of daylight, to wind velocity was different. Every day was a surprise that first year. We'd get used to one type of weather, and it would change without a minute's notice. The duration of the seasons even varied from year to year. I missed the long Swedish summer days that would stretch to midnight, but I liked the show of sun during Kansas winters that we didn't see in Sweden.

And the endless expanse of sky—I was awe-struck with it. It was an immense showcase of strength that no one could overpower. It blanketed the earth, giving it comfort or punishment, as the weather dictated. Our livelihood depended on farming the soil, but it was the sky that would decide what we would reap from it.

The wide sky is a brilliant blue now, with not a cloud in sight. And earlier this morning we wondered if it would clear at all today.

I think early autumn is my favorite time of year. Its not too hot or cold, windy or stormy. The balmy days gradually warm up to a comfortable temperature but cool down to wonderful sleeping weather. I could stay outside all day today.

Our farm comes into view as we slope down the last hill, then disappears a moment until the next rise. The barn and outbuildings are instantly visible, but we can only glimpse the house even though it is on top of the land. The trees we've planted around the house over the years have secluded it.

We hastily built shelter for ourselves and the farm's needs the first seasons. The dugout was our home for three years until we built the first section of our house. Crude outbuildings of cheap lumber didn't last long. Before the first decade was over we improved or replaced most of them.

The place has a settled look to it, being more than five decades old, but it doesn't have the strength and durability of the stone and log timber farm compound we had at Kulla in Sweden. Planks of American cottonwood lumber just aren't as strong as Swedish pine logs. Built a century or more before we left them, those old buildings were sturdy enough to be used for a long time to come.

We planted trees every spring on this place those first years. We even dug holes and set saplings around the "house" before the house was even built. A few had to be moved after our home was started, but I couldn't wait to get some shade growing. Our first trees were little twigs dug up from the creek and river banks. Fruit trees were grown from seeds saved from the fruit we had bought and enjoyed. Later we bought trees from stores in town or traveling tree peddlers.

We were never ever to duplicate the feeling of the Swedish forest with our Kansas grove of trees, but they have provided fruit for the family and a wind break for our homestead.

Just as we are about to turn in our homestead, Gilbert appears over the hill in his Studebaker car coming from the east. He waves, then turns to follow us into our driveway. He pulls in to face opposite us, turning off the motor so we can hear each other. Gilbert opens the car door, and our dog leaps up on his hind legs to greet him.

"Mother! Good to see you out enjoying the weather today. How many bushels of corn did you pick?" He is teasing me

Gilbert

because I'm still clutching the corn stalk that's been riding as my companion throughout the countryside.

"Do you want to come in for dinner?" asks Samuel.

"No, thanks. I've been to town for supplies and just wanted to stop in a minute. Esther will be expecting me home soon."

Probably the handsomest of my sons, I consider him the most outgoing and friendly of our children. He always has a smile on his face and an easy conversation for everyone he meets.

Gilbert was my fifth child but grew up to be known as the third in the line of Johnson children since we buried two babies before he was born. Oscar and Emily were nine and seven when he arrived. He was a tag-along until Teddy was born three years later and grew to become his playmate.

Growing up on the farm made his vocational choice of farming himself an easy one. Gilbert's first corn harvest was spent in a makeshift cradle in the seat of the wagon. I was working in the field too, so it was natural to bring him along. The next few years, as he started to toddle and then walk around, he wandered between the rows, playing hide and seek as we worked. Eventually he looked after Teddy, then Esther, in the wagon, then graduated to picking corn himself.

Gilbert and Teddy were always following Samuel and Oscar around the farm. The boys were too small to fit into the older men's steps, but they tried so hard. They wanted to grew into their elders' hats and boots, and their chores too.

Even though they were separated when young, Gilbert and Teddy had happy times together on this farm. From friendly water fights in the horse water tank to playing ball in the garden with a tree limb and an under-ripe pumpkin, they had fun between doing their chores.

I remember the first time Gilbert drove the team of horses by himself. He was so small he wouldn't have been able to hold back the pair if they decided to take off, but the animals sensed they had a young driver in charge and behaved themselves. The men were cutting broom corn, and Gilbert and Teddy brought a load of stalks to the farm yard.

I could tell my son was scared, but he had such a large smile on his face. He had been given a grownup task and had accomplished it.

Now living nearby, we see him often during the week. He stops in to check on us, or we see him and his wife, Esther, at church functions.

Gilbert married a neighbor girl, Esther Miller, in her father's home in 1904, and they moved onto Gilbert's farm a few miles to the north and west of the church.

We've known the Millers since the beginning of the start of Salemsborg. Esther was Mrs. Miller's seventh child, but she died when Esther was five months old. The baby was raised by her oldest sister, Mary, who married my daughter-in-law Albertina's brother, John Anderson. So the Johnson, Miller, and Anderson families often are together for holidays and reunions.

Gilbert and Esther has a large house with beautiful furnishings and often hosts the family gatherings or church groups. Their natural ease makes their home a fun one to visit. My son and daughter-in-law were not blessed with children, so they share their time and talent with the church and community instead. But Gilbert would have made an excellent father. Instead he has doted on his nephews and nieces when they were grow-

Esther Miller

ing up. They always loved to go stay with "Pa," as he's called by the young ones, because they knew they would have fun there.

This son is the one who has kept this family together. Whether the situation is happy or sad, he makes sure everyone is

Their wedding, May 19, 1904

Gilbert and Esther's farm

there to celebrate or mourn together. This will be important, because before long Sam and I will be gone. And after all the sacrifices it took us to bring and raise our family here, I'd hate for our children to drift apart.

Church group meeting at Gilbert and Esther's home

39

Esther and Abraham's wedding, February 28, 1907

Delaying for Sunshine

Daughter Esther has dinner on the table by the time we finish visiting with Gilbert in the farmyard. When she moved back in with us three years ago, she needed the distraction and took over the cooking and cleaning for me as my health deteriorated.

She's an efficient homemaker. Having had no children of her own, she concentrated on her home and farm while she lived there with her husband. She grew enough garden produce on her place to fill both of our cellars. Tidy flower beds surrounded her porch. She even mowed the grass with a push lawnmower.

Every time she came over for a visit during the summer, she would have a few jars of something newly preserved. Samuel had his heart's desire for choices of jams. For a while it accumulated so much that he started eating it by the spoonsful out of the jar, knowing she'd have something else to share the next week.

Esther was always the little mother to the younger boys, to the point of being bossy when they teased her too much. Of course they grew out of it, but now, decades later, it seems at times as if the three of them are slipping back into the same routine.

As a child, she was the one who took care of the sick animals on our farm. Whether is was bottle feeding an orphaned calf, treating an injured horse, or checking in on hatching chicks, she took over the care of the animal that needed help.

A tall, thin girl with average features, she blossomed when Abraham Thelander started paying extra attention to her. She's

Esther

always been shy, and I was afraid it would be hard for a man to court her. Soon they were going to socials together, seen as a couple, and I was proud to see his hand on her elbow, or her's at his. Abe was so attentive and polite to her.

Abraham Thelander was an intelligent young man with a promising future. He was a prominent member of the church and the secretary for the telephone company for five years. His parents were close friends, with whom we had worked through good and bad times during our early days on the prairie. Abe was their only son, and they doted on him.

Abe farmed his parents land and his own eighty acres adjacent to them. Abe bought more land over time and was considered a wealthy farmer in our area. He built a new spacious home for Esther before the wedding, and it looked as if it would be a wonderful life for her.

We had a house full of family and neighbors for their February wedding in 1907. It was a union of two families who had worked together since the beginning of our community. The preacher performed the ceremony in the parlor, and we celebrated with a feast I remember preparing for days before the event. We celebrated the good fortune of our daughter.

The Thelander Family

I remember her smile that day. She beamed with quiet beauty in the exceptional gown she had designed and sewn just for the event. All the hard work I had done for my children seemed to have paid off that day. Everything I had dreamed of for my child had come true.

Unfortunately the outcome of my younger daughter's life was forever altered by the man she married.

They were married a few years, then something went wrong with Abe's mind after a minor accident and the operation to correct it. His first spell lasted a few months, and he spent most of his time living outdoors, terrorizing travelers by stepping out in front of people as they passed on the road. Abe was finally caught, sent away to get help for his mind, and seemed to be recovered when he came home again.

Then little things started to happen again. He'd seem fine at times, yet at others he would drive around the country with his car loaded with guns, making threats to people he had known for years. Abe was arrested on one of his jaunts and taken into custody by the county sheriff. He had become too dangerous to have at home or in the community. He was put on trial, found to be insane, and committed to seek treatment in September of 1915. He was home again after a few months but had to be re-admitted again the following March.

Oh, the embarrassment Esther felt because of Abe's actions. She wasn't the one insane, but people talked. She left more than one church service in tears. Cruel jokes were made hinting that she was the cause of his condition. Abe's problems weren't hers, but the stigma attached was. She continued to live alone on the farm, getting help from her family with the planting and harvesting. Her circle of friends dwindled. She couldn't do anything with the couples who used to associate with them.

Her mother-in-law had died two years before, and Esther had taken over the care of Abe's father, bringing him meals, checking in on him. He was shunned too, so they both were often missing from church socials.

Then the next October of that year, the Saline county sheriff came to Esther's house to notify her that Abe had escaped from the sanitarium in Kansas City. They didn't know where he was but guessed that he would make his way back to the area if he could. Esther, not daring to be home alone, moved in with Emily in Lindsborg.

Two weeks later, on a Friday night, Abe was spotted in the neighborhood. My sons and neighbors, armed with guns, combed the buildings on the Thelander place looking for Abe that night. He couldn't be found, but it turns out he was in the house. Ted had searched it earlier but had missed his hiding place. I still shudder at the thought of what could have happened if Abe had confronted him.

Oscar and my grandsons went back home, but Ted and Edgar took turns watching for Abe from the upstairs windows, worried that their crazed uncle might make his way to their house when he found out that Esther had left. Joseph and Herbert did the same here. We didn't know what Abe would do this time. And it made sense that one of our homes would be among the places he'd check for Esther.

The sheriff approached Esther's house the next morning only to greeted by a violent Abe, flashing guns and vowing not to be taken alive. Deputized men kept a close watch on the house for hours to prevent his escape but dared not get close because Abe fired at the posse throughout the day.

Finally about midnight the sheriff threatened to dynamite the house if Abe didn't surrender. Instead, Abe set the house on fire himself with gunpowder. When the muffled roar burst the house into flames, Abe raced out the front door past the surprised men. The search was on again until he was spotted near his father's place the next morning. Abe was finally captured in the pasture between the two farms after two men wounded him with bird shot.

Abe was taken into the county jail in Salina. He asked for Esther, but she was too upset to see him. The desperate man next wanted five thousand dollars from his father so he could leave the country. But he was sent to the state asylum instead. It had been a year since Abe's first committal, and gossip had died down. Now it started up again as word spread of Abe's attack. Curious people drove by to see the burned house. Talk returned

Esther's house before it burned down

to haunt Esther once again as the story was detailed in the newspapers.

Nothing was salvaged from the burned structure. Clothing, household items, the beautiful glassware collection in her parlor—all were gone.

Esther lost everything in the fire except her insane husband's name and the misery he caused her. Only this time she had no home to retreat to. So, Esther moved back into her old bedroom here in this house.

A new house has been built on her farm, but she decided she didn't want to live there anymore. I think she would always be haunted by Abe's return. Instead, she rented out the farm to her nephew and his wife.

It has been an embarrassment that has made it hard for her to hold her head up. She is legally married to an insane man and is tied to him until one of them dies. Divorce has been suggested, but then she wouldn't own the farm anymore.

We have all felt the humiliation that Esther has endured these last years. Her brothers have become protective again, just as they had been when she was a little girl getting bullied on the school ground. Her life has been put on hold, like a harvest being delayed because it needs more sunshine to dry the crop. Unfortunately, this marriage is a disaster than can not be salvaged when the weather clears.

West side of Sam and Charlotta's house

Back side of Sam and Charlotta's house

Estimating the Bushels

I slowly wander through the house after dinner. I go from chair to table to chair to wall, anything to lean on for balance.

I hear the spring on the porch screen door doing its job, slapping shut as Joe heads out the dining room to the west porch. He probably won't be back in the house again until lunch time.

Herbert is on the back porch hauling up a pail of water from the enclosed well. Being the youngest, he inherited the chore when he was old enough to lift the bucket. Decades later he still does it for the family. Esther emptied the hot water reservoir on the stove to wash the dishes from our dinner meal, so he is refilling it for her.

I used to dry the dishes for Esther, but it got to the point that I was too weak to grasp the wet dishes. After breaking the third plate, I resigned my job. I decided I was more help by not helping.

New bread loaves rest under a tea towel on the counter of the side table. Two flies, attracted to the scent, roam the top of the cloth.

The kitchen is hot from this morning's baking. The weather outside is moderate today, but you can't tell that by this room. Esther baked enough loaves of bread to last us the next several days, and pies for tomorrow's dinner. She tries to prepare food a little ahead on Saturday, so there is not as much work in the kitchen on Sunday.

How many meals have I prepared in this kitchen over the years? And how many hundreds of pies, jars of preserves, barrels of pickles? I've sweated my weight here preparing food for the family, sifted tons of flour. Gravy spoons have worn out, dishes have been broken, crocks cracked.

When was the last time I made a meal without help? What did I prepare? I had recipes, favorites of the family and for which I was known in the neighborhood. I smile with satisfaction as I recall my watermelon pickles and fried chicken that always disappeared first at church picnics. I made a chocolate cream pie that the men drooled over. The crust was thick but delicately flaky; the filling extra rich and smooth; and I always topped it with a high meringue. I never told anyone, but I added baking powder while beating the egg whites so the meringue was never tough. It was my signature dessert when we had harvest workers. Sam used to say that's why he never had problems finding neighbors to come over to help. They knew they would get all the chocolate pie they could eat.

I reach the doorway into the parlor and stop to survey the room. Samuel has fallen asleep in his favorite chair. The latest newspaper is draped across his lap, slipping from his grasp when he dozed off. He'll eventually return to his reading when he has rested, but the scenario will repeat itself all afternoon until it is time for coffee again.

Herbert's latest reading material is stacked on the table beside the rocking chair. Both boys love to read, but especially Herbert. Classics are his favorite, while Joe leans more towards the news and anything he can find on agriculture. Both can read Swedish and English, so both languages may be in the house at once. I'm afraid that I never caught on to the American language very well, but I never thought I needed to because we all still speak Swedish in the community. Some words I recognize, but reading through an article in a English newspaper, I find it is almost impossible to translate all the words. I didn't know how to read at all until I learned with my children. Girls in Sweden weren't trained in reading and writing unless you were from a rich family that hired a tutor.

I'm glad that all my children, boys and girls, got a good education, and I was very proud when the two youngest attended

Salemsberg Star Band

Bethany College for the commercial class. These opportunities of education will benefit them for the rest of their lives.

Joseph's trombone and Herbert's cornet cases lean up against the wall in the parlor, there until the next time they play, which I think will be on Monday evening, their practice night. Two folders of music are tossed on the settee. One music sheet looks like it's ready to slide out onto the floor, so I ease by the front of the couch to rearrange the stack.

Joseph and Herbert play in the Salemsberg Star Band. This amateur group plays any time they are called for concerts, whether it be for church or a farm sale. Most towns around here have band groups. Joseph also plays in the Falun Orchestra.

Family members have been well represented over the years since the Salemsborg band formed. Oscar and Gilbert played in it before they were married. Grandson Ted plays in it now, as does Albertina's two brothers John and Alfred—and Ed Miller, Esther's brother, and half of the neighborhood boys.

In the early years of the band, the boys would ride horseback to their meeting place and oftentimes strap the instrument cases

Falun Orchestra

on their backs, or carry them under their arms. Some men would ride together, one person picking up others in his wagon on the way to the concert or practice, thus having a vehicle to haul all the instruments. On their way home, they might play their instruments, and we could hear them going by on the road in front of the house. We couldn't see them in the dark, but their tunes drifted up to our bedroom window. Then we knew the concert was over and our boys should be on their way home.

We try to go to as many concerts as we can, depending on where they are. Sometimes we go early with Joe and Herbert, or Oscar or Gilbert provide our transportation. Samuel's hearing has diminished, but he can hear the band just fine. His foot and his hand on his knee keep time with the rhythm. And of course he's also there for any refreshment they may be serving afterwards.

Our piano sits with the lid closed to keep out the dust. After Emily married, it wasn't used much. I don't play, and Esther has never had much interest in it. I can usually talk Adelia into playing the latest piece she is working on when she comes to visit.

With difficulty I sit down on the piano stool. I reach for the worn hymnal that rests on the rack and open the cover, slowly turning the pages looking for familiar songs. I use a hymnal in church every Sunday but rarely use the one here, unless I want to look up something for reference.

I silently hum along in my head as I encounter favorite songs, scanning verses I know by heart, reliving the feelings that they evoked when they were sung at important moments during my life. Songs for the church holidays, communion, and mourning. How many funeral processions I have walked in over the decades, for family of my own or for dear neighbors?

The charter members of our church have dwindled drastically over the past decade; we have all grown old. I try not to think that Sam or I might be next that the young people talk about. "Remember old Mrs. Sam Johnson? Well she died today, and her funeral is Wednesday." "Is that so? I thought she was already dead!" I remember being young and thinking that I would never become as old as the elders in our church. I'm afraid my time will come soon.

As I turn the pages I find the song we sang as we stood beside the graves of Teddy and Almeda. It was a somber song, reflecting the sorrow of death, but with a ray of hope in the last verse, because the dearly departed is in heaven with God.

How very hard that day was. Joseph had just been born less than two weeks before these two children became ill and died within a day of each other. I'm glad that Joseph and Herbert didn't have to go through the trauma of losing their siblings, but at the same time, they missed the cherished years we had with them.

Death can be horrible at the moment it happens, depending on the circumstances, but it can also bring peace for the dying. It's a part of life that we must accept. And as I struggle with my afflictions, I am almost ready for that peace myself.

What songs would I like sung at my funeral? Two favorites come immediately to mind as I think of the part of the hymnal to which I'd turn to find them. I'd like Adelia to sing, and also the church choir, since one usually has a funeral at the home and again at the church.

"To the Glorious Land" comes to mind first, and also "There Will Be No Parting." The family might add some other songs, but I think they know these two are well liked by me and would be a comfort to Samuel.

Moving around the room I come face to face with the large portrait of my family.

How will my family remember me? I've looked so old for so long, I don't think they remember their youthful mother's past. My hair was not always gray, my back stiff, my speech impaired. Now I'm thought of as the ailing old lady, someone who has to be taken care of. They forget all the years of nurturing I did for them.

I wearily lay my hand against the wall to steady myself when I think of all the hard work I used to do around the farm. And bearing ten children meant I was pregnant for several of those years.

I have put my shoulder in the harness beside the one horse we had to help her pull the plow when she struggled through the sod. I have carried water long distances before we drilled our own well, hauled heavy bags of seed wheat unloaded from the wagon. It was just part of homesteading and working on the farm. The times Samuel was away working I had no choice but to do the labor myself. The animals still needed to be fed, the fields tended, and family cared for.

Matching oval frames on the west wall portray Joe and Herbert as young adults. These oil tinted photos of them were done at the same time we had a tint of Sam and me done, about five years ago. The portrayer used our images from our 1899 group photo but took new shots of the youngest boys because they had grown up since that picture was taken. Separated from the older children by a wide span of years, we treated our two youngest children almost like twins. And they have done everything together since they were little. Jobs around the farm still show their teamwork. Joe shovels left-handed and Herbert uses his right to clean out grain from the wagon together. They may do certain jobs by themselves, but each is doing a part that makes the task complete.

Joseph

Their young memories of their mother must be very different from those of Oscar and Emily. I no longer needed to be working in the fields, except on occasion, by the time they were born in the late 1880s. Herbert's cradle was a pillow and towel tied in the seat of the rocking chair in the kitchen instead of the box seat of the wagon. They weren't "introduced" to harvest until they were old enough to tag along to the field to actually be of help.

I turn the handle of the north parlor door and walk out on to the porch. Not often used as the entrance, this door is more for show. City strangers think this is the main door to the house, but country folk know to go to the west side porch. The only time neighbors have used the parlor door has been to enter for funerals and weddings. Weeks may go by, especially during cold weather, when we don't use this door at all.

We didn't do it every Sunday, but when the house was new, Samuel liked to drive the team and buggy around to the front of the house and collect us for our ride to church. May was always my favorite month to do that. I loved walking all dressed up through the blooming lilac bushes that lined the

Herbert

Front of the Johnson home

path out to the waiting buggy. It meant we had fulfilled a promise made when we left our home in Sweden. Someday we'd have a nice house and enjoy the trappings of a wealthy family. Well, we've never been close to rich in terms of money, but our dreams for our family have been fulfilled with this Kansas farm.

This porch was built for decoration, but it has served its purpose too. How many times have I come out on this porch to check the weather? The house sits on the highest part of our farm, and it always gave the best view of the approaching storms until the trees grew tall enough to block the scene. Then we'd climb out the upstairs window onto the roof of this porch, to check to see if we needed to scurry down to the cellar instead.

The slightest breeze fans my face. I tug at the collar of my blouse to undo the top button. I want to feel the air and warm sunshine on my throat.

I lean against the railing, breathing deeply to capture the scents of nature. The nectar of the ripening pears from the orchard next to the house mix with the pollen of the fall-blooming wildflowers that grow on the edge of this block of trees.

Gingerly I ease down onto the first step, then the second, as I make my way off the porch. Trying to balance myself, I work my way around the east side of the porch railing to the house siding. As luck would have it, a yard rake has been left leaning against the wall on the corner. Esther has been using the rake to gather the fallen fruit and has left it handy to use again later today. Perfect! Now I have a walking stick to help me get around the yard. I want to get past the trees that surround it.

The prairie grass to the north is starting to show a wave of gold in its hue. It is always subtle at first, then changes overnight with the first hard frost. From green to gold then to brown as the grass dies back for the winter. I've always felt sadness when the color left the stems, but I took comfort knowing the roots were resting for the next spring's show of color.

I can't believe how long we've lived on this land. The years have gone by so fast. It seems as if I could turn around and see the dugout again.

I've seen so many changes on the prairie when I stop to think back over the decades. First it was pure native grass, untouched until man moved in to homestead it. Then it was plowed and planted with the first crops. It was a battle between man and nature the first years until the grass roots were worked enough times that it died out. From then on the rich earth let us plant and sow grain crops instead.

I hope the land will continue to yield for generations to come. A good farmer will watch for subtle signs of overuse. We learned to fertilize the fields to put back the nutrients the plants used out of the soil.

But I wonder about all the new machinery that has been invented. They make farmers want to push the land's use, and the land may have a limit. Which generation of my farming descendants will see the change as the earth wears out like it did in Sweden?

My eyes sweep down to the northeast corner of our acreage. Fifty years ago we stood on that corner and surveyed our new land. Our hopes were planted there with our first crop of rye.

Not long after that it became a grave site. The bones of my babies still lie buried under its sod. I'm sure the crude wooden coffins we lovingly laid their bodies in decayed long ago. I no longer remember their individual features, but the images of their little sunburned faces paled by death have not faded from my memory.

The death of a child was a regular tragedy for many of our homesteading neighbors. Crude conditions in the dugouts and the absence of a doctor, medicine—or money for either—made it more heart-breaking. Knowing that some of the deaths could have been prevented if there had been a regular income—or if the family had lived in an established town—made some people leave their claims. For them the land wasn't worth the pain it had caused. To look out over the prairie and face another daunting day of work and memories was too much, and the immigrants traveled back to where they came from.

There were people who moved back to Sweden, but they were few in number. Even though we all thought about it at times, we couldn't afford to leave. That would have taken money, and we had spent it all getting here.

So we stayed, prayerfully estimating the bushels it would take from the fall's harvest, to survive the next year.

Praying for Yield

I'm back in my bed, not many hours after arising, it seems. My energy wanes after dinner so I must rest to continue the day. It is more comfortable to be here propped up in bed than sitting in a chair, so I spend many hours here. If I feel up to it, I look at a book or photos between dozing.

Life is depressing when one has to spend so much time in bed, separated from the activities of the home and farm. I have no choice but to accept it. I'm not the type to take my own life, although fleeting thoughts have strayed in that direction when emotions about my disabilities became overbearing.

I'm restless this afternoon. I'm uncomfortable, having problems with my meal settling. I'm feeling weaker than usual, but not sleepy.

So I decided to get my mind off my physical problems with things from my past to entertain myself this afternoon. Book albums and the family Bible, lie in a pile beside me.

I hear the honking of a car horn. That sound is as familiar now as the neigh of a horse or the jingle of the harness used to be. I crane my neck, trying to look out the window at the fleeing vehicle, but the flutter of the curtain prevents me from seeing who it is.

Used to be people could walk or ride a horse by the farm, and we'd never know to look up. Now everyone is announced whether or not they want to be. We can travel from one end of the county to the other in half the time it took us by horse and buggy. Our world has been expanded by the automobile. And as long as the weather and roads are clear, we can travel anywhere there is a road.

At one time, errands to Salina were only for necessary supplies when we could afford them. Sam would haul butter and eggs in to trade for goods that couldn't be raised on our farm. He made the journey, and I stayed home with the family. Or neighbors picked up supplies for several families on a trip.

Then Lindsborg, Assaria, Falun, and Smolan grew business districts that made shopping handier. Our trips shifted and came more frequent over the years.

Now we shop first at the cluster of stores west of our church because it is closest, and we want to support our local merchants. Before mail was delivered to our own mail box, we'd collect our letters at the general store on our way to church services.

These days people travel not only for supplies but to sight-see and discover what lies beyond the boundaries of our county.

Our community has grown in spurts. It was an empty plains for centuries except for Indians roaming the area. We came with a group in 1869, then other immigrants joined us as they left the old homeland. Faint trails became wider, dividing the country into a grid of permanent roads. Now telephone poles run along the ditches to connect our neighborhood door to door to area townspeople and merchants.

Families prospered, and this helped the growth of our communities. And it continues as many of the second and third generations stay on to farm the land we homesteaded for them.

Of course there have also been setbacks in the community over the years. Some, but not all, have been weather related. Smolan was demolished by a tornado in 1892, but the townspeople rebuilt. Droughts and low prices made financial disasters for many in 1888 and 1896.

I think of the recent war with Europe. I thought we would always be isolated in the country, but modern times have crept in. We kept up with news from the war front almost as if we were there ourselves. Our congregation had an intense reason to keep track of the situation because thirteen young men from our community served in the military. All but the Frost boy returned safely.

I reach for the fortieth anniversary album book of the Salesmborg church. The church is the basis of this community, both social and spiritual, so this was an important book to own. The gold letters embossed on the dark red cover are refined and elite.

We've built two more churches since the first crude sod dugout structure where we used to worship. The new spire church, completed in 1893, is so grand it has a cathedral interior and gas lights.

Leafing through these pages is a nostalgic journey through the development and changes that have happened over time. Two groups, the Assaria and Smolan congregations, split from us, and pastors have been replaced. The church park, complete with a band stand, was built and expanded for congregational picnics. Three horse barns were added for the protection of the animals and the vehicles they pulled to church.

Groups of all ages, from Sunday School to Bible groups, congregate at the church in the evenings during the week. Baptisms, confirmations, and burials have been administered before the altar. Countless prayers—from healing the sick, to increasing the yields, have been said from the pews.

Salemsborg Lutheran Church

Samuel and I are pictured in the charter members section. Our children and their spouses are featured in group poses.

Where is the section of memorial pictures of the deceased members of the congregation? I thumb through the pages until I reach the first page of this chapter. There are four or more photos on each page with the person's name and birth and death year printed underneath. I study each picture, remembering the people

Salemsborg Church Congregation, 1909

and how I was associated with them. Some people died young; others, such as the Larson brothers, were in the prime of their lives. Oh yes, their mother's photo is also featured. She died the next spring after her sons. And of course the older generation— Brodines, Sandbergs, Thelanders, and many others, who were our neighbors and friends in the beginning.

Not everyone who died during the past forty years is pictured. Some people might been mentioned, but there were no photos available for them. And others preferred not to be reminded of their deceased's passing with a photo in a book. We didn't add our children's photos, because we only had their casket pictures.

I open to the center that features a two-page spread of the whole congregation. I move my magnifying glass slowly up and down the rows as I recognize individuals and couples. Some families tried to sit together, but others are scattered in the photo. We're in the bottom left section of the photo with Oscar, Gilbert, Esther, and their families above us. Joe and Herbert are with the single men toward the top. Ted is with classmates.

I remember the day that photo was taken. It was after church service one Sunday, and it took so long to get the group seated. But it was exciting to capture our whole congregation in one photo. We started out as a very small group of immigrants, and I'm proud to say we've been a part of this community the whole time. Just this past May we celebrated our church's fiftieth anniversary.

I close this book and reach for the family Bible. Worn with years of use, the cover is about to fall off and a few pages have become loose inside.

Tucked in the front is a piece of paper. I unfold it to find our church transfer paper. It is dated May 2, 1868. That's the day we met with our Swedish pastor to fill out the paper saying we were leaving his congregation for America. Sam's and my names and other records are listed on two halves of the front, and Oscar and Emily are listed on the back.

The impact of our decision to leave Sweden sunk in that day as the pen was dipped in the ink well and drawn out to sign our names to that paper. We had cut our ties with our church, and there was no turning back.

I wonder what life would have been like if our transfer were not granted. Would we have tried again later? Gone without the church's blessing? Would we have stayed, becoming the old couple living in the farm compound in Kulla, while Oscar tried to eke out a living on that rocky patch of land? Or would we still be alive? Our life on the prairie was hard for the first decade, but conditions were still better here than in Sweden during that same period.

I absent-mindedly thumb through the pages, stopping now and again to read passages that have been marked—favorites of the family, or verses memorized for catechism.

One Bible Scripture has been repeating in my mind all day. I turn to 2 Timothy to find the verse.

"I have fought the good fight, I have finished the race, I have kept the faith."

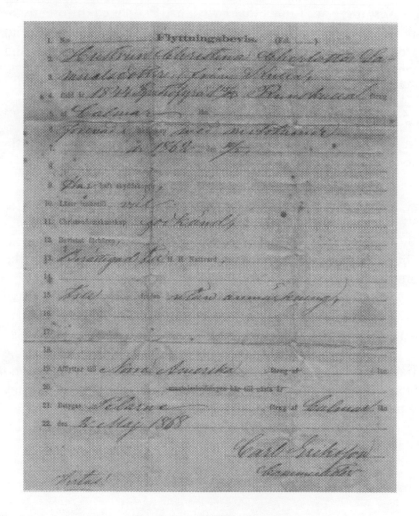

Charlotta's church transfer

I mull this over as I read it again. It fits my current situation.

"I have fought the good fight"—I have battled to provide for my family.

"I have finished the race"— my body has deteriorated to the point that my life could soon end.

" I have kept the faith"—overall I'm satisfied that I've done the best I could for my husband, family, and God.

It is a comforting verse. I close my eyes and breathe in deeply, feeling a sense of relief from the troubled presence of mind I've had today.

Yes, there are things that I wish had happened differently in my lifetime. I can relive the questions that haunted my mind throughout my life, but it still will not change the outcome and events that shaped our family's lives.

Natural disasters wipe out crops.

A drop of rain at the right time can save a plant that will feed a family for a meal or for a month.

A near accident one second missed could have altered a life one way or the other.

Disease can kill anyone, in body or in mind.

Life must be accepted the way it is. When young we rely on our parents and family for comfort, protection, growth, and knowledge. As we mature we take the responsibilities and help others. As we age, we rely on the younger generations of the family to take over the cycle and take care of us.

We must keep faith that all will work out as planned. I have worked toward survival and goals, but fate still has the ultimate hand in the outcome.

I close this chapter and return to the front of the Bible. In the first few pages of the book Samuel has written our names and the dates of the important events in our lives. He noted the day each time a child was born or died.

I trace my name, stopping with my birth date, December 15, 1844.

What date will be listed for my death?

Testing the Grain

Esther set my requested box of letters beside me on the bed. When she checked in on me, I asked her to fetch them from my dresser. It took some motioning for her to figure out what I wanted, but by pointing to the bottom drawer, shaping my hands into the size of the box I wanted, and scribbling in the air with an imaginary pen, she figured out that I wanted the old correspondence.

It has been many years since I've looked at the bundles of letters I had stashed in the drawer. Today I felt like reading them again. Right now they look all tidy and sealed, but these closed volumes always bring a flood of memories when opened again.

I can tell the decade the letters were written by the discoloration and condition of the paper. Early letters were pages folded to make their own envelopes; later ones had their own. Foreign stamps and ones from this country. Flowing cursive script and scratchings. Each one tells who the author is and when it was written, middle age growing old, or youngster growing up.

The brittle letters from fifty years ago are few in number but very precious and read so often they are yellowed and stained from handling and tears.

We wrote to our parents as often as we could afford the first years here. They did the same until they were unable.

We rarely heard from Samuel's family after his parents died. The contact was gone. I encouraged Samuel to write his brothers and sister, but it was a task that was hard for him to do it seemed, so I quit pestering him about it. It was his choice to let the years slide by.

We have sent pictures to Sweden over the years, but our siblings in Sweden rarely reciprocated.

I urged Sam at least to acknowledge one letter, dated 1900, from his sister. Samuel scoffed at her letter, saying she was exaggerating, but I thought it was a plea for help. Christina described the dire straits of their old farmhouse with the roof that was leaking, and she wanted Samuel to send her some money to fix up her place. Since he owned land in America, she thought he should have plenty to spare for her. Little did she realize land payments were due here also, even when the weather did not produce a good yield.

His sister also asked if we knew where her daughters were. Two of Samuel's nieces spent time with us after they arrived in America, but they soon moved to California and married. It has been years since we heard from them, and apparently it was the same for Christina. Either way, as a mother, I can understand why it was distressing to Christina.

I think of my own sisters, Hedda and Mathilda. I was so lucky that they decided to move to America when we did. It helped ease the separation of family and home in Sweden. Pictures of

Hedda and her family, 1880s

them and their families are cherished because they are both gone now.

Hedda and her family lived nearby until moving to Washington state in 1896, and then later to California. I saw her only a few times after that, but we religiously wrote back and forth. Hedda died three years ago and is buried in California. I miss her postcards boasting the fruits of the state. Her daughter occasionally writes, so we keep track of Hedda's husband and children that way. None of them settled back in this area.

Mathilda and Lars moved to Lindsborg and built a grand house in 1910. Lars wanted his children to go to Bethany College and was ready to retire from the farm, so they left the Enterprise area. Lars died five years later at age eighty-seven after he fell and broke his hip.

Mathilda passed away by accident a year ago in August. As far as we could tell by evidence, she fell down the back curved stairway that led to the kitchen, crawled into the dining room, and managed to get on the chaise lounge. She was home alone at the time. Oscar Lofgren eventually found her, but it was too late. She was only sixty-eight and in good health, but apparently her internal injuries were too great.

Their son Thure now teaches voice at Bethany and lives in his parents' house with his

Mathilda and her family, 1880s

family. Julia, his older sister, and her family farm the original homestead at Enterprise. Their other sister, Lydia, met a visiting preacher who was in Lindsborg for a convention, and she plans to marry him later this year.

Lars did well over the years, so they were able to travel back to Sweden to see family a few times. They never went all at once as a family but made separate trips, taking one of the children along each time. I wish I could have done the same, but I had to settle with Mathilda's stories instead. The same with Hedda and her far-off home. We never had the money to travel outside the state.

"Dear Lotta, Hedda and Tilda," I read in my father's handwriting. Even though he might vary to whom he sent the letter, he always wrote to all three of us.

More often than not, he asked questions about our families and farms, when we hungered for news about theirs instead.

"How did the winter wheat handle the cold weather you had this spring? Did frost damage the developing kernels? I'd like to test that variety of grain here. Would you please send a small packet?"

Seeds were sent back and forth, as a common link between the two places. I always felt like a child, filled with anticipation, when a bulky letter arrived from Sweden. What did Father send this time? During his final years, I think these letters, and their contents, kept father interested in living.

The faintest scent of pine mingles with the moldy dust of this old letter. Gray needles, once plucked from a fresh Swedish pine tree, still rest in the fold of the paper. They were added before the envelope was originally mailed and have been kept with the letter all these years.

The scent instantly takes me back to the hillside at our old farm in Sweden. I close my eyes, breathing in the clear scent of the resin, feeling the gentle spring breeze as it barely whistles through the trees.

Tinkle, tinkle, tinkle. The musical notes from the milk cow's bell ring from the distance. I can't see the cow below in the meadow, but I know she is close by. She is looking for a patch of grass to graze while waiting for me to milk her.

I sit on a large mossy rock, looking down on our farm below. The weather-beaten farm buildings stand tightly clustered together to form the compound that shelters our family, livestock, and the food needed for both.

I hug my knees to my chest, wrapping my arms around my bent legs, trying to keep warm against the early morning chill.

The hill rolls below me underneath the canopy of pines and of birch trees that have yet to add their spring leaves. Lack of rain fall has delayed their budding. Patches of rocks protrude here and there all the way down to the bottom, continuing throughout the fields where we try to raise our crops.

I am up here early this morning to think about the decision that was made last night. In my head I know we have no choice, but my heart is rebelling. Large numbers of Swedes are leaving to escape our country's troubles, and we're to be among them.

Surviving on the farm grows bleaker as the drought continued through the winter and into this spring. Without the much needed rain to replenish the ground's moisture, there is no chance of the next crop growing either.

I shut my eyes tightly to delay the stream of tears that I know is going to run down my face. Isn't there anything we can do to stay here? I don't want to leave our families and move to a foreign country!

Sam and I have discussed and argued about what we should do, among ourselves and with our parents. When we first married we had such big dreams about our future, but I can't imagine those dreams developing elsewhere, and without our family close by.

Free land in America became Samuel's big dream last year. At first I thought it was a way to shut out the dire conditions of this place, a way to cope with the situation. But he was thinking about America's land being the solution instead.

"Let's leave this place behind! It isn't providing for us. Why should be stay?!" he'd demand.

"We should stay because our family is here!" I'd hotly answer back.

69

"For our family—our children—is why we should go!"
He was right. Our parents had lived their lives and didn't
have many years left, but our children were just starting theirs—
if we would leave so they could survive.

Memories of my loved ones here bring me back to the present and make me reach for the photo album. Portraits are such wonderful mementos. I wish there had been such a thing as affordable photography when I was growing up. I would have loved to have taken portraits of our parents and grandparents with us when we left Sweden. Then I could have shown our children what their ancestors looked like.

Every now and then I see a glimpse of a past relative in my own reflection, or that of one of the children or grandchildren. My father's eyes shine in Gilbert's, and Esther's long face reminds me of Samuel's mother. I can comment on the similarity to that person, but with a photo I could have shown the resemblance and how important the past is in shaping our looks and personalities.

Our album features pitifully few photos of our children. We didn't have the money to spend on photos until they were older. Now I wish we had scrimped and gathered enough money together to have had a portrait taken when the children were little. I think how cherished a picture of Josephina and Axel would have been, or a family photo before Teddy and Almeda died. These were opportunities lost that I deeply regret.

Harvesting the Crop

"Want some coffee, Charlotta?"

Samuel startles me as he taps his cane on the footboard of our bed. I was engrossed in the album and didn't hear him shuffle into our bedroom.

"Charlotta, did you want some afternoon lunch? Esther has made chocolate pie."

I'm tempted, but I'm still thinking about Albertina's burnt sugar cake, and shake my head to answer no.

"What you looking at?" asks Sam as he wanders around to my side of the bed. He peers closer, then looks behind him, apparently deciding it would be easier on his knees if he brought a chair to the side of the bed. After a few seconds he is sitting beside me and has pulled the album closer to his eyes to look at the photo I have turned to.

"Oh, look at Hazel! She was a little doll in her first picture." He flips the pages, not studying them like I did, but enjoying them just the same. "And Ted with the little curls

Granddaughter Hazel

71

Grandson Ted

Albertina worked into his hair for his picture. I think he's still embarrassed of that photo.

"Oh yes, here's the one of Ted, Edgar and Hazel. This photo didn't show their true character. Their personalities were the exact opposite of what this picture represented. They weren't solemn little people when released outside to play."

I had already worked my way to the back of the album, so now Samuel thumbs toward the front of the book, going from the photos of our grandchildren to those of our children.

He turns sober when he spots Teddy and Almeda in their coffins. "I often think of the children we buried."

I'm taken aback by his admission. When was the last time the two of us talked privately about the children we lost? Maybe I hadn't realized that a father's loss could be as deeply felt as a mother's.

"What do you suppose they would have looked like grown up," he continues. "I think they resembled Joseph and Esther the most." And then he states matter-of-factly, "We would have had to buy more land for Teddy."

I wish I could add to this talk, but I can't. Yet Sam seems to fill in both sides of the conversation, musing out loud, reminiscing as he works through the pictures from Herbert to Oscar.

He taps a photo. "Remember when Gilbert built his house? I almost fell off the second floor when we were putting up the roof rafters."

I'd like to comment that he shouldn't have been up there in the first place, but his sideways glance tells me he knows what I'm thinking.

He holds up a recent photo of us that has been stuck between the inside front cover and the first page of the book. It hasn't been mounted in the al-

Ted, Hazel and Edgar

bum yet, although it was taken early this past spring. We were in Lindsborg, in front of Emily's house. Part of a Bethany College building shows up in the background corner because the trees haven't leafed out yet. It shows Sam and me in front of Gilbert's car, with our son and Esther already seated inside it.

"Look at us, Charlotta. Riding around in a college town in an automobile! Who would have thought when we walked out to homestead this prairie that we'd be doing this now?"

He tucks the photo back into its place and studies the first portrait in the album. It is a replica of the one sitting on our dresser, showing us and our children.

Sam is suddenly quiet, apparently deep in his own private thought about the sons and daughters born to us.

73

Charlotta and Samuel in front of Esther and Gilbert

"We've had some good and bad times on this farm, Charlotta," he observes, and then with pride he adds, "but I think the best crop we ever raised was our children."

He stares at the photo a minute longer, then carefully closes the album and sets in on the table beside the bed.

"Get some rest. After coffee we can start putting the hay up in the barn loft. And if you don't want to do that, you can get the wheat drill ready. We'll soon be planting wheat." I smile at his parting words, enjoying his gentle teasing.

In an unusual gesture, he leans over and gives me a kiss. "I'll eat your piece of chocolate pie for you," he says as he pats my shoulder.

I blow him a kiss as he heads toward the door.

Planting Dreams

"Esther! Esther! I can't get your momma to wake up!"

I hear Sam's voice in the distance, but I can't seem to open my eyes. I try to reach for his arm, but my hand won't move.

I hear their voices murmur above me, but I can't respond. The porch screen door slams shut, and I can faintly hear a high-pitched voice outside through the open window. Within no time the clomps of work boots enter the house and halt beside my bed. They are talking to me—about me—but I can't answer.

The evening light fades away from my sight but not from my senses. My eyes may never see the sun rise again, but I feel peace with this evening's sunset. I know the sun will always rise above the Smoky Hill Buttes to find this land.

I hope I have taught my children that faith must be continually renewed like the crops in the field. Like the grains of a harvest, faith will nourish them, but it is depleted and must be replanted again and again. There must be a next planting, tending, and harvest to continue life.

My well-being depended on the touch of the wind and sun, the sounds of the prairie, and the feel of the soil. Material possessions and people were lost over time, but this patch of Kansas earth always helped me cope with the sadness and turned my spirit around.

Even when crops failed, I could always count on harvesting faith from this land. . .

As I draw my last breath, I am planting my dreams into my children and my grandchildren.

I'm standing in the northeast corner of our farm, looking at our farmstead from a distance. I look over my shoulder to the east—toward Sweden, but turn back west to face our farm. I pick up the bucket of seed wheat by my feet and head home.
I'm ready to plant my next field.

Charlotta's funeral on September 17, 1919

DIED.

Mrs. Charlotta Johnson

Christina Charlotta Johnson, wife of Samuel Johnson, passed away at her home in Salemsborg, Kansas, on September 13, 1919, having attained the age of seventy-four years, eight months and twenty-eight days.

The deceased is survived by her husband, four sons and two daughters, also five grandchildren and a wide circle of friends. The children are Mrs. Emily Larson, Mrs. Abraham Thelander, and Messrs. C. O. Gilbert, Joseph and Herbert Johnson.

The Johnson family were formerly residents of our city and are well known in this vicinity.

Funeral services were held on Wednesday afternoon from the late home and from the Salemsborg church.

————O————

Charlotta's obituary in the Lindsborg News-Record

DÖD

—

Samuel Frederick Johnson

afsomnade i tron på sin frälsare i sitt hem i Salemsborg, Kansas, den 25:te oktober 1919 i en ålder af 83 år, 2 månader och 26 dagar.

Begrafningen äger rum onsdagen den 29:de oktober från sorgehuset klockan 2:00 och i kyrkan i Salemsborg klockan 2:30 e. m.

Vänner inbjudas.

Samuel's announcement of death on October 25, 1919

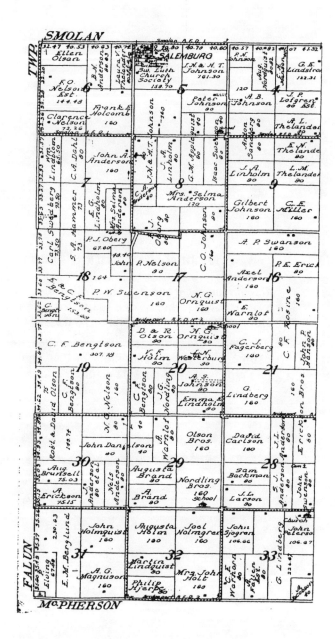

1920- Saline County, Kansas

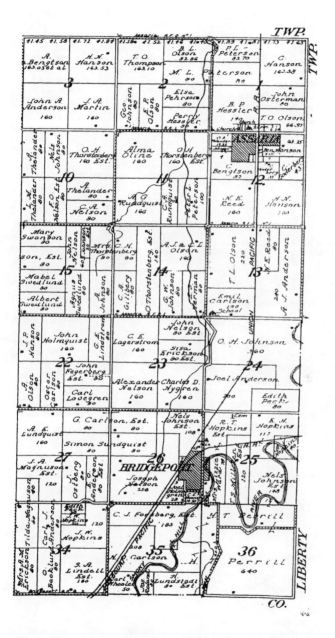

Township 16 South, Range 3 West (Smoky View)

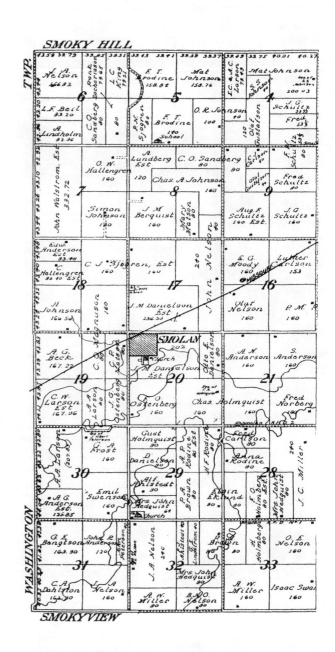

1920- Saline County, Kansas

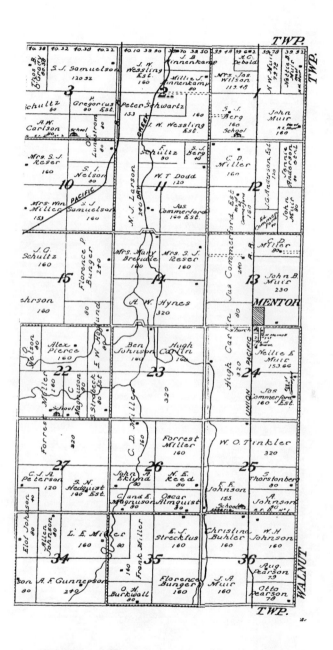

Township 15 South, Range 3 West (Smolan)

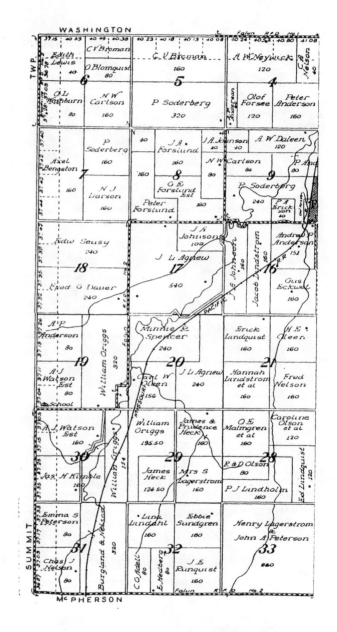

1920- Saline County, Kansas

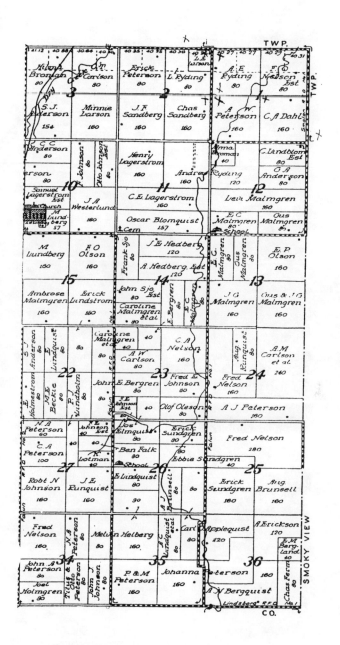

Township 16 South, Range 4 West (Falun)

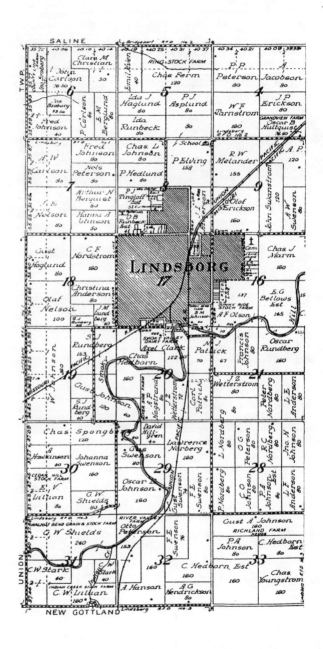

1921- McPherson County, Kansas

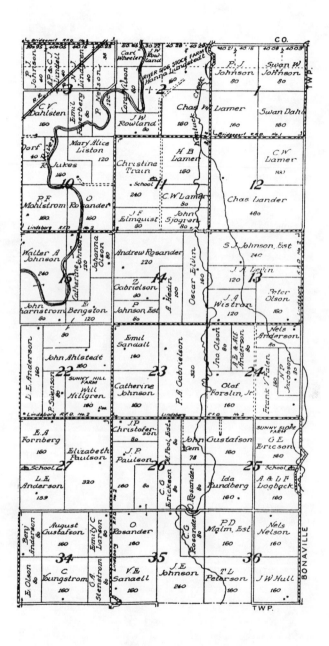

Township 17 South, Range 3 West (Smoky Hill)

87

Selected Bibliography

Andreas, A. T. *History of the State of Kansas*. Chicago, Ill.: A. T. Andreas, 1883.

Billdt, Ruth. *Pioneer Swedish-American Culture in Central Kansas*. Lindsborg, Kans.: Lindsborg News-Record, 1965.

Billdt, Ruth, and Elizabeth Jaderborg. *The Smoky Valley in the After Years*. Lindsborg, Kans.: Lindsborg News-Record, 1969.

Cochran, Edith, Walemar Dreivts and Mary A. Mattson. *Smolan, Kansas: A Century of New Horizons 1886-1986*.

Deaths and Interments- Saline Co., Kansas 1859-1985. Compiled by the Smoky Valley Genealogical Society and Library Inc., 1985.

Kansas Farmer & Mail and Breeze Reliable Directory. Topeka, Kans.: Kansas Farmer & Mail and Breeze, 1920.

Holmquist, Thomas N. Pioneer Cross. Hillsboro, Kans.: Hearth Publishing, 1994.

Lindquist, Emory K. *Bethany in Kansas*. Lindsborg, Kans.: Bethany College, 1975.

————. *The Smoky Valley People: A History of Lindsborg, Kansas*. Rock Island, Ill.: Augustana Book Concern, 1953.

————. *Vision for a Valley: Olof Olsson and the Early History of Lindsborg*. Lindsborg, Kans.: Bethany College, 1970.

Lindsborg Efter Femtio År. Rock Island, Ill.: Augustana Book Concern, 1919.

Lindsborg pa Svensk-Amerikansk Kulturbild från Mellersta Kansas. Rock Island, Ill.: Augustana Book Concern, 1909.

Minnes Album—Svenska Lutherska Församlingen, Salemsborg, Kansas, 1869-1909. Rock Island, Ill.: Augustana Book Concern, 1909.

Butter in the Well Series

Butter in the Well
Read the endearing account of Kajsa Svensson Runeberg, an immigrant wife who recounts how she and her family built up a farm on the unsettled prairie.

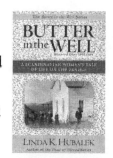

Quality soft book.   ISBN-13: 978-1-886652-00-2
6 x 9, 144 pages   ISBN-10: 1-886652-00-7

Prairie Bloomin'
This tender, touching diary continues the saga of Kajsa Runeberg's family through her daughter, Alma, as she blossoms into a young woman.

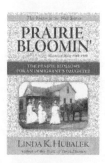

Quality soft book.   ISBN-13: 978-1-886652-31-6
6 x 9, 144 pages   ISBN-10: 1-886652-01-5

Egg Gravy
Everyone who's ever treasured a family recipe or marveled at the special touches Mother added to her cooking will enjoy this collection of recipes and wisdom from the homestead family.

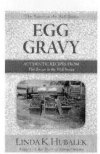

Quality soft book.   ISBN-13: 978-1-886652-02-6
6 x 9, 136 pages   ISBN-10: 1-886652-02-3

Looking Back
During her final week on the land she homesteaded, Kajsa reminisces about the growth and changes she experienced during her 51 years on the farm. Don't miss this heart-touching finale!

Quality soft book.   ISBN-13: 978-1-886652-03-3
6 x 9, 140 pages   ISBN-10: 1-886652-03-1

Trail of Thread Series

Find out what it was like for the thousands of families who made the cross-country journey into the unknown. "Stitch" your way across country with these letters and quilt diagrams from the 1800s. This series feature history from 1854 to 1865.

Trail of Thread
Taste the dust of the road and feel the wind in your face as you travel with a Kentucky family by wagon trail to the new territory of Kansas in 1854.

Quality soft book.   ISBN-13: 978-1-886652-06-4
6 x 9, 124 pages   ISBN-10: 1-886652-06-6

Thimble of Soil
Experience the terror of the fighting and the determination to endure as you stake a claim alongside the women caught in the bloody conflicts of Kansas in the 1850s.

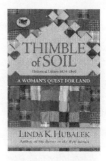

Quality soft book.   ISBN 13: 978-1-886652-07-1
6 x 9, 120 pages   ISBN-10: 1-886652-07-4

Stitch of Courage
Face the uncertainty of the conflict and challenge the purpose of the fight with the women of Kansas during the Civil War.

Quality soft book.   ISBN 13: 978-1-886652-08-8
6 x 9, 120 pages   ISBN-10: 1-886652-08-2

Planting Dreams Series

Drought has scorched the farmland of Sweden and there is no harvest to feed families or livestock. Taxes are due and there is little money to pay them. But there is a ship sailing for America, where the government is giving land to anyone who wants to claim a homestead. So begins a migration out of Sweden to a new life on the Great Plains of America. Can you imagine starting a journey to an unknown country, not knowing what the country would be like, where you would live, or how you would survive? Did you make the right decision to leave in the first place?

Planting Dreams

Follow Swedish immigrant Charlotta Johnson and her family as they travel by rail and ship from their homeland in 1868, to their homestead on the open plains of Kansas.

Quality soft book. ISBN-13: 978-1-886652-11-8
6 x 9, 122 pages   ISBN-10: 1-886652-11-2

Cultivating Hope
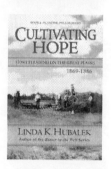
Through hardship and heartache Charlotta and Samuel face crises with their children and their land as they build their farmstead.

Quality soft book. ISBN-13: 978-1-886652-12-5
6 x 9, 130 pages   ISBN-10: 1-886652-12-0

Harvesting Faith

As her life draws to the end, Charlotta reviews the work and sacrifice of her family's years on the prairie, and the changes seen in her lifetime since leaving Sweden.

Quality soft book. ISBN-13: 978-1-886652-13-2
6 x 9, 112 pages   ISBN-10: 1-886652-13-9

Order Form- Photocopy or tear out page

Butterfield Books Inc.
PO Box 407
Lindsborg KS 67456-0407
Orders: 1-800-790-2665 **Office:** 785-227-9250
Fax: 866-227-6578 **email:** staff@ButterfieldBooks.com
Order online at www.ButterfieldBooks.com

Send to:
Name _____

Address _____

City, St, Zip _____

Phone _____ **Email** _____

☐ Check enclosed for entire amount payable to **Butterfield Books Inc.**
Charge to my: ☐ **Visa** ☐ **MasterCard** ☐ **Discover** ☐ **AmEx**

Card #: _____ **Exp.** _____

Signature _____ **Date** _____

ISBN #	Title	Qty	Unit Price	Total
9781-886652-00-2	Butter in the Well		11.95	
9781-886652-31-6	Prairie Bloomin'		11.95	
9781-886652-02-6	Egg Gravy		11.95	
9781-886652-03-3	Looking Back		11.95	
	Butter in the Well Series (4 bks)		42.95	
9781-886652-06-4	Trail of Thread		11.95	
9781-886652-07-1	Thimble of Soil		11.95	
9781-886652-08-8	Stitch of Courage		11.95	
	Trail of Thread Series (3 bks)		32.95	
9781-886652-11-8	Planting Dreams		11.95	
9781-886652-12-5	Cultivating Hope		11.95	
9781-886652-13-2	Harvesting Faith		11.95	
	Planting Dreams Series (3 bks)		32.95	
			Subtotal	
		KS add	8.8% tax	
	S/H per address: $3.00 for 1st book, Each add'l $.50			
			Total	

Retailers, Libraries, and Schools: Books are available through
Butterfield Books Inc., and book or quilt wholesalers.

Order Form- Photocopy or tear out page

Butterfield Books Inc.
PO Box 407
Lindsborg KS 67456-0407
Orders: 1-800-790-2665 **Office:** 785-227-9250
Fax: 866-227-6578 **email:** staff@ButterfieldBooks.com
Order online at www.ButterfieldBooks.com

Send to:
Name _____

Address _____

City, St, Zip _____

Phone _____ **Email** _____

☐ Check enclosed for entire amount payable to **Butterfield Books Inc.**
Charge to my: ☐ **Visa** ☐ **MasterCard** ☐ **Discover** ☐ **AmEx**

Card #: _____ **Exp.** _____

Signature _____ **Date** _____

ISBN #	Title	Qty	Unit Price	Total
9781-886652-00-2	Butter in the Well		11.95	
9781-886652-31-6	Prairie Bloomin'		11.95	
9781-886652-02-6	Egg Gravy		11.95	
9781-886652-03-3	Looking Back		11.95	
	Butter in the Well Series (4 bks)		42.95	
9781-886652-06-4	Trail of Thread		11.95	
9781-886652-07-1	Thimble of Soil		11.95	
9781-886652-08-8	Stitch of Courage		11.95	
	Trail of Thread Series (3 bks)		32.95	
9781-886652-11-8	Planting Dreams		11.95	
9781-886652-12-5	Cultivating Hope		11.95	
9781-886652-13-2	Harvesting Faith		11.95	
	Planting Dreams Series (3 bks)		32.95	
			Subtotal	
		KS add	8.8% tax	
	S/H per address: $3.00 for 1st book, Each add'l $.50			
			Total	

Retailers, Libraries, and Schools: Books are available through
Butterfield Books Inc., and book or quilt wholesalers.

About the Author

A door may close in your life but a window will open instead.

Linda Hubalek knew years ago she wanted to write a book someday about her great-grandmother, Kizzie Pieratt, but it took a major move in her life to point her toward her new career in writing.

Hubalek's chance came unexpectedly when her husband was transferred from his job in the Midwest to the West Coast. She had to sell her wholesale floral business and find a new career.

Homesick for her family and the farmland of the Midwest, she turned to writing about what she missed, and the inspiration was kindled thus to write about her ancestors and the land they homesteaded.

What resulted was the *Butter in the Well* series, four books based on the Swedish immigrant woman who homesteaded the family farm in Kansas where Hubalek grew up.

In her second series, *Trail of Thread*, Hubalek follows her maternal ancestors who travel to Kansas in the 1850s. These three books relive the turbulent times the pioneer women faced before and during the Civil War.

Planting Dreams, her third series, portrays Hubalek's great-great-grandmother, who left Sweden in 1868 to find land in America. These three books trace her family's journey to Kansas and the homesteading of their farm.

Linda Hubalek lives in the Midwest again, close to the roots that started her writing career.

The author loves to hear from her readers. You may write to her in care of Book Kansas!/Butterfield Books, PO Box 407, Lindsborg, KS 67456-0407.